# Betrayal

## Society Lost, Volume Two

## By Steven C. Bird

# Betrayal

## Society Lost, Volume Two



Published by Steven C. Bird at Homefront Books

Illustrated by Hristo Kovatliev

Edited by Carol Madding at hopespringsedits@yahoo.com

Final Review by Sabrina Jean at fasttrackediting.com

Print Edition 7.31

ISBN-13: 978-1535428682

ISBN-10: 1535428686

www.homefrontbooks.com

www.stevencbird.com

facebook.com/homefrontbooks

scbird@homefrontbooks.com

## Table of Contents

## Disclaimer

The characters and events in this book are fictitious. Any similarities to real events or persons, past or present, living or dead, are purely coincidental and are not intended by the author. Although this book is based on real places and some real events and trends, it is a work of fiction for entertainment purposes only. None of the activities in this book are intended to replace legal activities and your own good judgment.

## Dedication

With each book that I write, my list of people to whom I owe an enormous debt gets longer and longer. There are numerous individuals in the indie author community that help to make the dream of writing a reality for myself and many others. That list is, of course, too long to detail here, but for each and every one who has given me guidance or encouragement along the way, I owe you all an eternal debt of gratitude.

To my beautiful wife and loving children: may this book be only one of many more that I write that helps to secure our future together, living the life that we dream of.

## Introduction

## Continued from - The Shepherd: Society Lost

After leaving Spence and the rescued girls with Jörgen and the remainder of his group, former Sheriff Jessie Townsend traveled the new and unforgiving world alone and on foot, continuing his quest to find his sister.

Still suffering tremendously from the tragic and brutal loss of his family, Jessie walked the Earth, a prisoner of his own thoughts. Although each of his days had a purpose, continuing his quest that may or may not end before his death, Jessie felt a certain level of emotional numbness that only being alone could provide him. After his loss, as well as the other tragic losses of life he had witnessed since leaving his homestead high in the Rocky Mountains, Jessie enjoyed the solitude. He knew that the joys of friendship and love could lead to heartache and tragedy. No, if he died alone in this world, no one would have to shed a tear, no one would have to risk their life for his, and his choices would put only himself in harm's way. That cold and empty simplicity seemed to be a good fit for Jessie as he headed east into the unknown of what may lay ahead.

Although Jessie found solitude in his empty heart—solitude that he felt he desperately needed—not a day went by that he didn't think back to those whom he had encountered along the way. In this mad and twisted world, devoid of law, order, and the civility that people around the world had come to expect as the norm prior to the *great collapse*, Jessie knew that there were still good people out there. Good people who would have to face the evil that this lawless and dangerous new world had spawned, once the walls of society came crumbling down around them.

## Chapter One

As the modern day wagon train, consisting of two older pickup trucks and a minivan, worked its way west across New Mexico via Highway 60 toward Fort Sumner, the driver of the lead vehicle, Gavin Keene, squinted to see through the dusty windshield. The setting sun seemed to illuminate every speck of dirt that clung to the glass. Gavin, a thirty-three-year-old widower, and father of two small children, Patricia and Gavin, Jr., ages five and seven respectively, was the leader of a small group of survivors who had set out to reach the safety of the town of Fort Sumner, located just east of Albuquerque, New Mexico.

Having heard news of adequate supplies of food, water, and medicine being available there, by word of mouth, HAM radio transmissions, and an AM radio frequency they had discovered during their daily scan of the airwaves, Gavin and his group had decided to attempt the journey in order to build a better life for themselves and their children. They decided to risk everything, in an attempt to give their children a chance at the safety and security that they had been without for so long.

Gavin drove the lead vehicle, a 2003 Ford F-150 pickup truck with a fiberglass canopy shell covering the bed, pulling a small four-by-eight-foot utility trailer along behind. The trailer was heavily laden with the group's remaining possessions. He was joined in the cab of the truck by Russell Johnson, a man of Scottish descent in his late twenties, who had immigrated to the United States when he was a young boy.

The middle vehicle, a Dodge minivan, was driven by Brandon McCoy, a thirty-seven-year-old Navy veteran who had lost his entire family during the violence that had ensued after the collapse. Brandon had been hardened by his losses, and was a fierce and fearless defender of his group. It was this protective tendency that won him the lead position in the minivan, which carried both of Gavin's children, as well as Leina Sallander's eight-year-old daughter, Kayla. Leina rode along with Brandon in the minivan to tend to the children's needs during their journey, as well as being an extra set of eyes, looking for threats while Brandon drove. The minivan offered the children the most room to climb around and play together during the journey, as their stops would be brief and discreet.

Bringing up the rear were Adam and Becky Stoner, driving a 1999 four-wheel-drive Toyota pickup truck. Adam and Becky were a married couple who had lost their special needs child after the collapse, once her medical care became unavailable. Adam and Becky were the quick-response security team of the group. With their small, lightly-loaded and highly maneuverable truck, they were able to take up a defensive position with their vehicle, in the event the group came under attack. Both Adam and Becky were armed with AR-15s they had purchased before the collapse, when the government had first attempted to ban the private ownership of weapons. They had paid a substantial premium for the guns once the 'run-on-the-firearms market' had begun, but with the value of paper money now non-existent, they felt it was the wisest purchase they had ever made.

Looking over at Gavin, Russell broke the silence by saying, "I'd say we've got about an hour of daylight left. We should probably start looking for a place to spend the night."

"Yeah, I know," Gavin replied, struggling to see, blinded by the setting sun. "It's way too wide open out here, though. We need to press on and find some cover up ahead. I'd feel extremely vulnerable camping out in the open."

"Yeah, you're right. That makes sense. Let's just keep going," Russell replied.

"What's that?" Gavin asked, leaning closer to the dust-covered windshield in an attempt to get a better look.

"What? What do you see?"

"I could have sworn I saw a glint of light on the hill ahead and to the left. I can't see a dang thing, though, so who knows. It's probably fatigue."

As Russell reached down between his legs to retrieve his binoculars, he heard the crack of glass as the windshield shattered, looking over just in time to see Gavin's head whip back violently with blood and bits of hair and flesh splattering across the pickup truck's rear window.

The vehicle abruptly swerved to the left as Russell reached for the controls. Hearing several other metallic thuds from bullets impacting the hood, he kept his head down below the dashboard, hoping to straighten the truck's path while it slowed. His desperate attempt to grab the steering wheel was a mere second too late, as he felt the truck's tires begin to side-load, initiating a violent roll toward the passenger side door.

After what seemed like at least five successive rollovers, the truck came to a stop on its side with the passenger door to the ground. Quickly regaining his bearings after nearly being knocked unconscious by the violent force of the crash, Russell felt a warm liquid beginning to cover his body. Panicking at first, assuming that it might be fuel, he looked up to see Gavin's body hanging above him, held in place by his seatbelt, with blood oozing out of the massive head wound, dripping down onto him below.

Wiping the blood from his face, Russell could hear the sounds of gunfire coming from what he believed was the Toyota. Quickly looking around to find a way out, he pushed up on the now-crushed-in roof of the truck and began kicking the windshield violently, trying to knock away the shattered glass so that he could escape.

Once he had freed himself, Russell climbed through the windshield, quickly turning back to grab his rifle, a Ruger Mini-

14 Ranch Rifle chambered in .223 Remington, a cartridge that complimented Adam and Becky's AR-15s.

Hearing the occasional bullet impact the bottom of the F-150, which now lay on its side, Russell worked his way around the truck to the rear of the bed, making sure to stay low, in case any of the rounds penetrated the truck's thin, sheet metal body.

Looking back at the others, Russell saw that Adam and Becky had positioned the Toyota between their attackers and the minivan to provide the occupants of the van with cover. Russell could hear Brandon desperately trying to start the minivan, with steam now emanating from the vehicle's front grill and fluids leaking profusely onto the ground. Using his binoculars, Russell could see numerous bullet holes in the hood of the minivan, a sign that it had been intentionally disabled by their attackers.

~~~~

Giving up on getting the minivan running again, realizing that the damage was too severe, Brandon looked to Leina and said, "Get them outside along the side of the van. Keep them low."

Sliding his Romanian AKM with a shorted ten-inch barrel out the window, Brandon began to lay down a barrage of fire in the direction of their attackers, who they still could not positively identify as they were being engaged from such a long distance.

"Come on," Leina said to the children as she crouched down behind the van, reaching to them with her hand through the now opened door.

Slipping outside one-by-one to her protective arms, the children huddled together, terrified and crying.

Upon firing the last round in his thirty-round magazine, Brandon slid across the seat and behind the van with Leina and
~~~~

the kids. Quickly rocking a fresh magazine into place and cycling the action on his AKM, he said, “Here, take this. That pistol of yours won’t do you any good. Stay here with the kids. I’m gonna grab my .308 out of the trunk and give Adam and Becky a hand.”

Nodding in the affirmative, Leina took the gun and said, “Be careful,” with fear in her eyes.

Working his way around to the back of the minivan, Brandon opened the rear cargo hatch while trying to stay down and out of the direct line of sight of the shooters, who from what he could tell, had a position of elevation in the hills southwest of their position. This gave their attackers the advantages of both elevation and having the sun at their backs, their muzzle flashes remaining hidden in the blinding rays of the setting sun.

Making a break for the Toyota, Brandon left his position of cover and ran to Adam and Becky’s position. The Stoners were taking on heavy fire from the attackers, and Brandon simply could not just stand by and watch.

~~~~

Back at the truck, Russell felt helpless as he watched Leina and the children cowering in fear behind the minivan. He knew, however, that if he tried to make it the fifty-plus yards of open terrain to reach them, he would be picked off in short order. He had already seen firsthand how well placed their attacker’s shots were, even from such a distance, and he simply couldn’t take the chance.

As he watched helplessly from behind the overturned truck, he noticed Brandon dart from his position of cover behind the van and advance toward the Toyota. Russell’s heart sank in his chest as he saw Brandon flinch, slowing his pace, only to flinch
~~~~

again before falling to the ground, face down, as a pool of blood formed beneath him.

"Nooooo!" Russell shouted as he punched the side of the bed of the Ford in frustration.

He then saw Becky turn to run to Brandon's aid as Adam grabbed her arm and tried to stop her, only to have her, too, fall to the ground, her arm still in her husband's grasp. As Adam dropped to his knees before her in absolute shock, a high-velocity rifle bullet penetrated his back, sending him slumping over his wife's dead body, joining her in death's cold embrace.

Ducking back behind the Ford to avoid being the next victim, Russell felt his heart pounding in his chest as he watched from a distance as Leina and the children remained behind the van, totally helpless and vulnerable. Leina looked at him with tears in her eyes. They both understood that they had no foreseeable way out of this situation, and with their friends now dead, both Russell and Leina knew they were no match for whoever was raining hell down upon them.

## Chapter Two

It had been over a month since Jessie had left Spence and the others to continue his journey to find his sister. With the temperatures climbing as summer approached, he knew he needed to start traveling by night for more than just reasons of stealth.

Traveling by foot had given him plenty time to reflect on what had been, and what might be, of his life, allowing him to start to heal and come to terms with his losses. However, the rigorous nature of traveling by foot was starting to take its toll on him. He knew he needed to find a new mode of transportation and find it soon.

Climbing up to the top of a hill just east of Red Lake, Jessie found a suitable location to make his camp for the night. With adequate escape routes, as well as good long-range visibility, he looked around and said to himself, "This will do."

As he stretched a desert-camo canvas tarp over a length of paracord, anchored at one end to a nearby rock and the other to a tree branch, Jessie placed his pack on the ground, propping his rifle up against it.

Prior to Jessie's departure, Spence, unofficially knowing the mission and long, arduous journey his friend was about to secretly resume, sourced him a DPMS LR-308 patterned AR-10-style rifle, chambered in .308 Winchester/7.62x51 NATO, from the group's supply inventory. Spence knew that the contributions Jessie had made in his short time with them had more than covered the value of the rifle, and he would simply ask for forgiveness after Jessie was gone.

The rifle, equipped with a twenty-inch heavy profile barrel, a fully floated keymod forward handguard, a 4-12X Leupold scope with ballistic drop compensation, and a set of forty-five degree offset back-up iron sights, was more than capable of handling virtually any task or challenge that might come Jessie's way.

As Jessie leaned back against his pack, he pulled his journal from his pocket, clicked his pen, and began to make his daily entry.

*The dreams that once haunted me in my sleep appear to have faded away. Perhaps my mind is just too fatigued to entertain them. Though I feel more in touch with myself than I have in quite some time, I also feel detached. Detached from what? That, I do not know. All I know is that I am pulled toward a goal with an uncertain ending, like an actor in a play who is standing on stage, in front of the crowd, but hasn't yet begun to read the script.*

*As the seasons change, the days are growing longer, and the nights warmer. This is both welcomed and unwelcomed. I am pleased with the warmth the advancement of spring provides, but I know that the cover of darkness is a valuable thing, and as the summer progresses, it will be even more scarce.*

*Only having seen signs of people from a distance as of late, my travels have gone mostly unimpeded. Today, however, I came across several sets of relatively fresh vehicle tracks. It appeared the vehicles had passed through the area within the last day. Something to keep a look out for.*

*For now, it's time to rest my feet, feed my anxious stomach, and get some sleep.*

Placing his journal back into his pack, Jessie fished around inside and removed a cloth drawstring bag containing herbal tea. Placing a pinch of tea into his stainless steel, reusable tea infuser, Jessie dropped it into his stainless steel camping mug. Using his folding, portable rocket stove, he warmed the mug, now filled with water from his canteen, with the infuser inside. Almost immediately, the soothing scents produced by the simmering herbs began to waft up around him from the small, well-contained fire.

Taking a deep breath, Jessie thought to himself, *It's the little things, these days. Thank God for the little things.*

As he watched the last moments of the sun as it passed over the western horizon, Jessie took a sip of his hot, fresh tea. His moment of peace and serenity was soon disrupted as the sounds of multiple gunshots began to echo from the distance to the east. Lowering his cup, Jessie tuned his ears to the sounds, counting the shots, and noting the differences in sound. *Someone is returning fire,* he thought.

Looking back at the setting sun and then checking the time on his wind-up watch that he kept set to his own time based on the daily high noon position of the sun, Jessie thought, *it will be dark long before I could get anywhere near the source of the fighting. God, be with the innocents... if there are any.*

After a few moments, as the distant sounds began to fade, Jessie looked off to the west as the sun dipped below the horizon, and murmured to himself, "Well, it's over," as he lowered his head in respect for the dead. He knew all too well the inevitable outcome of any armed conflict. No one ever gets away unscathed.

## Chapter Three

As Russell and Leina looked to each other from a distance, both pinned down behind their vehicles, they heard a vehicle approaching from behind them on their exposed side, appearing out of nowhere from behind the rolling terrain. Russell placed his rifle on the ground and put his hands on his head, nodding for Leina to do the same. He knew there was no way out, and not knowing what their intentions were, he felt the best thing they could do for the children was to comply, even if for no other reason than to buy them some time.

As the vehicle drew near, they could see it was a Ford pickup truck with several armed individuals standing in the bed, weapons trained on them. Stopping just short of them, a man in the back of the truck shouted, "Lay face down on the ground, all of you! Hands and feet spread apart!"

Russell acquiesced to their demands, positioning himself in a way to keep his eyes on Leina and the children. He could see Leina trying to coax the children to comply, and could hear the sorrowful cries of Gavin's children as they yelled, "Where's Daddy? Where's Daddy? Daddy! Come get us, Daddy!"

Covered in their father's blood, Russell's heart was broken at the thought of the emotional hell the children were enduring, as well as the potential horrors that awaited them all.

His thoughts were quickly interrupted as the man who had given the previous order, said to the other two men in the bed of the truck, "Get on it."

*Get on what?* Russell thought as the men climbed down and began walking toward them with their rifles trained on both him and Leina.

Walking toward them were two men in their early to mid-thirties with athletic builds. They were both wearing black tactical web gear, body armor, and police-style tactical Kevlar helmets with identity-hiding face wraps. The men were well armed with AR-15 rifles, adorned with high-end optics, targeting lasers, and tactical lights. Watching as the men searched the dead and took their weapons, Russell could tell this was no simple misunderstanding or case of mistaken identity. These men were well-equipped and trained marauders—the type that carved out their niche in this chaotic and dangerous world, preying on the weaknesses of others.

Sifting through the contents of the vehicles, one of the men turned to the apparent leader, still standing in the back of the truck, and shouted, “It’s clear, and we got a good one this time.”

Jumping down from the back of the truck, the man who seemed to be in charge of the group looked into the cab of the truck as he walked by and said, “Call the others in.” Proceeding to walk over to his cohort who had called clear, he said, “What do we have?”

“The big score is the woman and the kids, of course, but they were also pretty heavily armed, so their ammo and weapons will carry some value. They also had at least a two-week supply of food.”

“Outstanding,” the authoritarian figure said. “Put the women and the children in the Suburban,” he said pointing to several vehicles that were approaching from in front of the group’s bullet-riddled trucks and minivan. “Put the food and anything else of value in the Jeep. Let’s wrap this up quick and get back. I’m getting hungry,” he said, pausing to look at Leina. “And I’m anxious to get to know the woman better,” he added with a devious, crooked smile.

“Sure thing, Chief,” one of the men said, as he immediately turned toward Leina and the children. Pausing, the man then asked, “What about him?” he said, gesturing toward Russell.

"What about him?" the one they called Chief replied sarcastically and with an annoyed tone in his voice.

"Yeah, right," the man quickly responded, as he realized the answer to the question was self-evident.

His heart pounding, unsure of what was about to transpire, Russell watched the man turn toward him, as what appeared to be a Chevrolet Suburban equipped with police lights, a brush guard, and multiple radio antennae arrived, with a Jeep Wrangler following several car-lengths behind. Both the Suburban and the Jeep had been painted a flat desert tan color with splotches of brown, in what appeared to be an attempt to blend in with the surrounding terrain.

The men in the Suburban exited the vehicle and began talking with the man referred to as Chief. Unable to hear their quiet conversation from his position, Russell saw the Chief point at Leina and the children as the men turned and began to walk toward them.

His attentions now back on the man who had been directed to deal with him, Russell's thoughts flashed back to his previous life. His mind raced as he wondered how he could have gone from an upper-middle-class American life as an aspiring pianist and composer, to being on the run in a collapsing world, his friends lying dead all around him, and his fate now in the hands of those who had killed them.

As the man walked toward him, grasping his sidearm, still in its holster, the Chief yelled, "Don't waste ammo."

Stopping and nodding to acknowledge the order, the man proceeded toward Russell, his right hand now shifting from his sidearm to a large knife worn on his police-style duty belt.

His heart pounding in his chest, Russell began to sweat profusely as he saw the blade being drawn from its sheath. *No! No! No!* he thought as he looked to Leina, who was being taken away with the children and led in the direction of the Suburban.

Looking back to Russell, Leina silently mouthed the words, “Fight! Fight!” as one of the men nudged her in the back with his rifle, forcing her forward.

Focusing on the knife in the man’s hand, Russell cringed at the thought of the horribly painful death that awaited him. He couldn’t help but think of the burning sensation he would feel as the knife sliced into his flesh. *I’m not going out like this!* he thought as he immediately lunged forward to his feet, letting out a primal scream as he ran full-speed toward his would-be assailant.

Feeling the knife slash through his left shoulder as the man tried to thwart his attack, Russell pushed through the pain, grabbing the man’s Glock 17 from its holster. With another slash of the blade across his face, his vision now going blurry, Russell pulled the trigger repeatedly as the man tried to block the weapon with his free hand.

Falling to the ground on top of his assailant, everything seemed like it was moving in slow motion around him. Gunfire erupted from all directions. Feeling impacts all throughout his body, but no pain, Russell said a silent prayer for Leina and the children as he slipped off into darkness, leaving behind the hellish confines of what had become his life on Earth.

## Chapter Four

As Jessie approached what appeared to be an abandoned town, he carefully scanned the area for any signs of movement or potential threats. He worked his way forward, from building to building, pausing to listen and observe as he went.

Approaching what appeared to be a former middle school, he looked at the empty swings and merry-go-rounds on the playground that would have once been filled with the sounds of children, laughing and playing on such a beautiful day as this.

Suddenly, the silence was broken as he heard the screams of a young girl as she ran out from behind the school, followed by the sounds of barking, as what appeared to be a pack of feral dogs viciously pursued her. Immediately bringing his rifle to bear, Jessie flipped off the safety, took aim at the lead dog, pulled the trigger, and... click. Nothing. Hand-cycling the rifle's charging handle, ejecting the failed round and chambering the next one in the magazine, Jessie pulled the trigger only to once again hear the sound of the hammer falling forward onto the firing pin, followed by silence.

"Damn it!" he yelled as he dropped the rifle and took off running toward the girl, the dogs now leaping on top of her, tearing at her clothes and biting into her flesh as her screams filled the air.

Awakened by the sounds of a bird screeching overhead as it glided gently on the morning breeze in search of its first meal of the day, Jessie squinted as the sun sent its first rays of light over the eastern horizon. Jessie awoke to only the sounds of flourishing life all around him and the feel of the cool morning air. No dogs, no desperate screams of a young girl. With birds chirping all around him, Jessie said aloud, "Crap!" as his heart rate began to slow down, realizing it had only been a dream.

Sitting up and getting a good look at his surroundings, Jessie stretched and yawned as he shuffled his hand through his pack, thinking, *what a way to start the day. Oh, what I would do for a cup of coffee.*

As he laced up his boots and put his arms through the straps on his pack, Jessie couldn't help but think of the sounds of gunfire he had heard the evening before. With an intent to parallel Highway 60 from the north side as he traveled east, Jessie looked over the hill and thought, *I'd better stay on my toes. It seemed like the shots came from that direction. I'll know soon enough, I guess.*

~~~~

After a half hour of carefully moving toward the east, pausing regularly to glass the surrounding area with his rifle-scope, Jessie saw several vehicles up ahead. With his scope on its maximum zoom, Jessie counted three vehicles, but they were still at too great a distance for him to make out any specific details.

Working his way toward the vehicles, Jessie thought, *I haven't seen them move yet, and I don't believe that they would have just camped out for the night in the middle of the road.*

Carefully working his way closer, using the terrain as cover, Jessie looked through his scope once again, only now he could clearly see the scene. *Two pickup trucks... a van on its side... damn it,* he thought, as he began to count the bodies strewn about the vehicles. *Bodies... of course, there would be bodies.*

After remaining in place for another hour to observe for movement, Jessie scanned the area off in the distance, looking for any glint of light reflecting off an optic, or any other signs that the area was being surveyed from afar. Once he felt it was safe to move about, having not seen or heard anything outside of
~~~~

nature, Jessie moved from his position of cover, which was just northwest of the vehicles, to an area to the northeast.

Jessie again sat patiently, watching and listening for any signs of trouble. He then moved in a southerly direction toward Highway 60. Once he reached the edge of the road, he left cover and sprinted across Highway 60 to the southern side of the road, where he worked his way from east to west, positioning himself to the southwest of the vehicles.

Having worked his way all around the area, Jessie was finally satisfied that the vehicles were not being watched. Standing up, exposing himself above the terrain, Jessie slowly and methodically worked his way toward the ambush site, keeping a keen eye out for trouble. The last thing he needed was to end up joining the poor souls lying on the ground in front of him.

Reaching the overturned F-150 that had come to rest on its passenger side door, Jessie looked inside to see the body of a man in his thirties hanging from his seatbelt, a thick, coagulated puddle of blood on the passenger side door beneath him. *Judging from these handprints and smears of blood, someone got out through the busted windshield,* he thought, as he tried to piece together the grizzly scene.

Lying just fifteen yards from the truck, Jessie found two dead men. A fair-skinned man in his late twenties with reddish hair, and another man, dressed in tactical gear, lying together in a pool of drying blood. Gently rolling the man in regular clothes off to the side, Jessie looked at the slashes across his face and cringed, noticing that one of his eyes had become dislodged during the apparent struggle.

Searching the man in tactical gear, Jessie found that he had been stripped of anything useful. No weapons or ammunition could be found, which seemed to indicate that there were survivors. Which side those survivors are on, of course, remained in question. *My guess is either the other guy's buddies or the attackers stripped this one clean before they left,* he thought.

Jessie then began searching the other vehicles, as well as the other bodies that remained at the scene. He found two other adult men and a woman. *Damn,* he thought, shaking his head in disgust. Sifting through the remaining contents of the minivan, Jessie noticed several children's toys, coloring books, and clothing. The coloring books, along with their associated crayons, were scattered around the back seat area as if they had been recently in use. In addition, a small pair of slip-on shoes, belonging to what Jessie assumed was a child aged six or seven were lying in the floor area of the backseat, with a pair of pink socks balled up neatly next to them.

Upon this discovery, Jessie knew in his heart that there had been children in this convoy, and they had been taken. His heart began pounding in his chest at the thought of what the children might be going through at that very moment. The fact that the children had not been killed at the scene with the adults told him that the perpetrators of the ambush had plans for them, which might keep them safe for now. Your average roadside bandit would not want to take on the job of caring for and feeding young children. Not for long, at least. No, there was more to this, and he wanted to know what.

Noticing that the fuel caps had been removed and left dangling from the vehicles' fuel tanks, Jessie said aloud to himself, "Looks like they took the gas. Except for the truck on its side," he noted, since the fuel cap was on the driver's side of the vehicle, just out of reach.

Walking around to the exposed underside of the truck, Jessie rapped on the vehicle's plastic fuel tank with his knuckles noting the deep thud instead of the empty hollow sound that he had expected to hear if the tank had been drained. "Here we go," he said.

Looking at the three vehicles, observing the bullet-riddled hood of both the minivan and the severe damage done to the Ford during the rollover, Jessie inspected the Toyota and thought, *this one might do it.*

Jessie then opened the driver's side door and brushed the bits of broken glass and other debris from the preceding battle onto the floor. He climbed inside, put the truck's five-speed manual transmission in neutral, and said aloud to himself, "Here goes," as he turned the ignition key.

Instantly coming to life, Jessie put the truck into first gear and began to ease out on the clutch to test the function of the vehicle as it shuttered to a stop, out of fuel. "Yep, they siphoned every last drop," he said as he scanned the instrument panel.

Quickly putting a plan together, Jessie searched the truck's bed to find a small, folding shovel amongst the now-deceased occupant's belongings. "Oh, yeah, this will work."

Unfolding the shovel and locking the blade into place, he walked over to the Ford and started digging holes underneath both of the passenger side tires that rested hub down and on their sides. Digging out all of the loose dirt around both tires, creating a hole where the tread of the tire would rest if the truck were to be upright, Jessie stood back to go over everything in his mind and said, "Yep, that should do it," as he tossed the shovel aside.

Next, taking a rope from the bed of the Toyota, Jessie tied the rope to the driver's side frame rail of the Ford. He pulled it through the roll bar mounted in the bed of the Toyota, and said, "Here goes," as he began to pull on the rope as hard as he could, bearing into the ground with both of his legs churning with all his might. Using the smooth, round tubular roll bar as a makeshift pulley, Jessie gained enough mechanical advantage to tip the Ford toward the holes he had dug underneath the wheels, causing it to fall back to the ground and land on all four tires.

As the Ford slammed its driver's side tires to the ground, the dead occupant's severely injured head smashed violently into the side window, splattering blood and body fluids on the glass. "Ahhh, jeeezzz," Jessie said as he surveyed the mess.

"Okay, I've got one running vehicle with no gas, and one non-running vehicle with gas." Jessie stared at the two vehicles and the remaining items left behind by those who had ambushed them, trying to come up with a way to move the fuel from one vehicle to the other without a container to carry it in.

After a few moments of pondering while scratching his chin, Jessie came up with a plan. With the Toyota's transmission still in neutral, he turned the steering wheel to the right, in the direction of the Ford. With the door open and his left hand on the driver's side window pillar and his right hand on the back of the cab, he pushed the truck, getting it to roll toward the other vehicle. Once he got the Toyota within a few feet of the Ford, he opened the hood of the Ford and popped the fuel line loose at the inlet for the fuel-injection system. Next, using his knife, Jessie scavenged several pieces of vacuum line from the truck and minivan's engines, piecing it together with splices he made from two-inch-long pieces of metal tubing scavenged from various systems. With approximately four feet of line, he squeezed the vacuum line onto the fuel line that he had removed from the Ford's fuel injection system and ran his makeshift fuel-transfer hose into the fuel-filler inlet of the Toyota.

Next, to stretch the energy in the Ford's battery as far as he could, using a ratchet sourced from a tool kit he found in a bed-mounted toolbox, Jessie removed the spark plugs from the Ford's engine, allowing it to spin freely without the burden of compression.

"Here goes," he said to himself as he turned the key on the Ford. As the starter began to turn the engine, the truck's mechanical fuel pump pumped the now-diverted fuel from the tank, through Jessie's patched-together transfer line, and into the Toyota's fuel tank. "There we go," he said.

Noticing a small leak from the pressure in the line at one of his splices, Jessie stopped cranking for a moment and tightly wrapped some scavenged electrical wire around the splice and tied it off securely, tightening the fit. Resuming his pump-assisted fuel transfer and observing no further leaks, Jessie continued transferring fuel until the Ford's battery was fully depleted. Quickly swapping out the Ford's battery with the one in the minivan, Jessie completed transferring as much fuel as he could, test started the Toyota, and then shut it back off, saying, "Now, to adequately address a few things."

Carefully and respectfully loading the bodies of the dead into the back of the Toyota, Jessie covered them with a blanket he had recovered from the back of the minivan. As he stood next to the truck with the door open, Jessie looked around and saw a hill off in the distance that would give a good vantage point of both sunsets and sunrises. He then drove the truck to the top of the hill, said a silent prayer, and spent the next two hours digging graves for each of the dead.

Once the bodies had been respectfully interred, Jessie placed his hat on top of his head, and with resolve in his heart, he climbed into the truck and set out in search of the children that he believed had been taken in the ambush. Still being a father and a sheriff in his heart, regardless of his losses, Jessie simply would not be able to live with himself if he didn't at least investigate the situation to the fullest extent of his abilities.

## Chapter Five

With Leina's arms wrapped tightly around the children, the Suburban sped down the road in the middle of the convoy, which from what she could tell, was heading in a westerly direction. She did her best to try and keep the children calm. Devastated by the loss of their father, young Gavin and Patricia clung tightly to Leina, crying the most sorrowful cries. "Daddy. I want Daddy," Patricia repeated over and over. With no words to comfort the children, Leina simply held them tight and let them cry. Overwhelmed by the fear of what might come, thoughts raced through her mind.

Looking around inside the vehicle, Leina noticed that it had previously been used in some sort of law enforcement capacity. The two men in the front seats, as well as the two sitting in the third row, directly behind her and the children, were all wearing the same desert tan tactical gear and clothing. They were obviously a well-organized and equipped group. She also noticed that they operated in a very disciplined and precise manner, as if they were professional soldiers of some sort.

Afraid to speak, Leina listened carefully to the men in the front and their muffled conversation.

"The chief wants us to bring the woman to him after we clean her up," the driver said to the man in the passenger seat.

"Of course, he does," the other man said in reply. "We do the work and he has the fun."

"Yeah, but at least we can have fun getting her all cleaned up," the driver said.

"Table scraps," the other man replied dismissively as he looked back to see Leina listening in. Flinching at her in an aggressive manner to intimidate her, the man smiled with satisfaction to see her recoil in fear. He turned back to the driver and said, "What about the kids?"

"Phillips and Lopez are supposed to take them to El Paso to see what they can get. They ought to be worth a few kilos each. Especially the girls."

"What?" Leina shouted, unable to contain herself any longer. "These kids aren't going anywhere! Who the hell do you think you are?"

Interrupted by a smack to the side of her face by one of the men in the rear seat, Leina's head whipped back violently against the seat as the man grabbed her by the hair. "Shut up, b——" the man said through gritted teeth.

"Hey, Lopez, no bruises," the man in the front passenger seat said. "The chief likes his ladies to look nice."

"Sorry, Barnes," the man said as he released his grip on her hair.

The one called Barnes then looked at Leina and said, "Stay calm and quiet, and things will go a lot easier. You give us trouble, and you'll get trouble. Understand?"

Replying with a nod, Leina clenched her teeth to refrain from unleashing her rage on the men. Turning her attentions to the children sitting beside her, Leina leaned over and kissed each on the forehead, and said, "It's gonna be okay. I won't let anything happen to you."

Barnes chuckled at her statement and then turned his attention back to the road ahead.

~~~~

Huddled up with the children in the middle row, Leina felt the Suburban begin to decelerate. Sitting up to see what was going on, she saw a small town off in the distance, directly ahead of them.
~~~~

As the vehicles approached what appeared to be a checkpoint with two armed men standing guard, dressed in the same gear as her captors, they were waved through without incident. As the vehicles drove through the town, Leina noticed an absence of activity. There was no one out and about. It appeared as if the town was entirely abandoned. Then, out of the corner of her eye, she saw a curtain in the window of a small one-story house draw closed, almost as if someone inside had been watching them drive by.

As the vehicles turned onto a side street, they pulled into the rear parking lot of a two-story block building. The parking lot was surrounded by a tall chain-link fence topped with razor wire, with security cameras mounted high above at each corner. Inside the parking lot, there were several of what she assumed to be police vehicles, all painted various shades of brown and tan. Once all three of the vehicles were safely inside the fenced parking lot, the gate was closed behind them by a man who was standing guard over the facility.

Coming to a stop, Barnes turned and looked at Leina, saying, “Don’t be stupid. Do what you’re told and things will go a lot smoother. Resist, and you’ll only make things harder on them,” gesturing toward the children.

As the driver placed the transmission in park and shut the vehicle off, he and Barnes exited the vehicle and walked around beside each of the rear doors. Barnes opened the passenger-side rear door and said, “Okay, you come with us. Phillips and Lopez will take care of the kids.”

“I’m not leaving them,” Leina said as she hugged the children tightly.

Without further warning, Barnes aggressively reached inside the vehicle, grabbing Leina by the foot, pulling her out of the Suburban as the children slipped from her grasp. As she was violently yanked out of the vehicle by Barnes, the children screamed in terror as the driver reached in for them from the other side. Attempting to grab onto anything she could to fight back, Leina's upper body slipped off the seat as she fell to the ground, the back of her head hitting the door-jamb of the vehicle and the pavement below, turning her world to darkness.

## Chapter Six

Driving west in the direction that the vehicle tracks suggested, Jessie passed Red Lake off to his right and thought to himself with frustration, *I can't believe I'm backtracking. I don't even know where the heck it is that I'm going, or what it is that I am even looking for. What's wrong with me?* he thought as he scanned the nearly flat terrain for an opportunity to gain the high ground for a vantage point. "Damn, I miss the mountains," he said as he saw a narrow dirt road leading into the small, barren hills behind Red Lake. "Looks like this will have to do."

He steered the truck off the main road. Tapping on the fuel gauge, he said, "Well, that's not gonna do for long," noting the insufficient amount of fuel he had obtained from the damaged Ford pickup.

As he brought the Toyota to a stop, Jessie removed the keys and slipped them into the side pocket of his light brown, cargo-style pants, placed his well-worn, wide-brimmed hat on top of his head, and stepped out of the truck, rifle in hand.

Walking further up the hill, with the town of Fort Sumner beginning to come into view, Jessie ducked down and crept to the peak of the terrain. Arriving at the best vantage point he could get, Jessie crawled to the edge and glassed the area below with his rifle's scope. *Too far,* he thought as he shifted his attention from the distant town to the roads of the surrounding area.

Patiently watching for movement down below, he noticed a trail of dust being kicked up behind a vehicle off in the distance. Focusing on the movement, Jessie dialed the parallax adjustment on his scope to infinite, in an attempt to fine-tune his focus for a better look. *Damn it,* he thought, frustrated that he was too far away to learn anything specific about the vehicle and its occupants.

Jessie's journey east on foot had taken him well north of Fort Sumner and then back south again to intercept Highway 60. *I went a long damn way out of the way to avoid this place, and now here I am,* he thought, second-guessing his decision to investigate the scene of the ambush.

Startled by an angry voice, Jessie heard a man say in an aggressive and forceful tone, "Hands off the gun, you thievin' son-of-a-b—!"

Knowing he couldn't turn around quickly enough from the prone position, Jessie reluctantly relaxed his grip on the rifle and gently placed it on the ground, saying, "I think we may have a misunderstanding here."

"There's no damn misunderstanding about it. You no-good looters and thieves have been coming to rustle my cattle for too long now, and I'm about to put an end to it!" the man shouted.

"Cattle? Sir, I have no idea what you're..."

"Shut up!"

Realizing he was losing control of the situation, Jessie began to slowly stand and turn around to his left, in an attempt to keep his holstered Colt out of plain view.

"Damn it, I said don't move!" the man shouted, cycling a round into the chamber of a Marlin model 1894 lever-action rifle.

Seeing a disheveled, elderly gentleman standing in front of him, wearing mismatched boots, torn pants, and a heavily soiled plaid button-up shirt, Jessie attempted to rationalize with the man who was clearly in distress. In a calm voice, he said, "Sir, I don't even know where your cattle are. I just came up here to try to get a look around. I didn't realize I was trespassing."

"You took my ranch, you took my family, and now you want to take what's left of my cattle! I won't stand for it! I won't take it! I'll kill you, you son of a b—!" the man shouted at the top of his lungs as he raised the rifle.

Seeing the psychotic rage in the man's eyes, Jessie quickly turned and drew his Colt as he attempted to move out of the man's line of fire, "No! Sir, don't! Don't!"

The almost silent tranquility of the calm desert evening was shattered by the crack of the man's rifle, followed immediately by the report of Jessie's Colt as the two guns discharged almost simultaneously.

Impacting the ground with his right shoulder, kicking up a cloud of dust, Jessie watched as the man fell backward as if in slow motion, his head bouncing on the hard dirt below and his rifle striking the ground just out of his reach.

"Damn it! I said no!" Jessie exclaimed as he rushed to his feet and to the man's side. Quickly looking him over for other weapons, Jessie removed the man's knife and tossed it aside. Seeing the fear in the dying man's eyes, Jessie said softly, "I didn't want to do it. I'm sorry. You left me no choice. Why couldn't you just let me be?"

"You bastards have taken everything from me," the man said, interrupted by a gurgled cough as his lungs began to pool with blood. "You... you've taken everything from me."

"I'm not whoever it is you think I am," Jessie said, looking into the man's eyes. "I know you're in a lot of pain. I know you've gone through a lot. But it's over now. You're about to be free from this world. Your suffering is over. I'm sorry. I'm truly sorry," Jessie said as he watched the man's last breath escape his lungs as he looked up to the heavens above.

Punching the ground in frustration, Jessie shouted, "Damn it! Why? Why? Why? Why did you make me do that?" He scooted back from the man and sat on the ground, looking up at the sky as if he was searching for answers.

Hearing a noise off in the distance, Jessie scrambled over to his rifle, picked it up, and began scanning the area below with his scope. “Crap!” he said as he saw two large SUVs speeding down Highway 60 toward his location.

Knowing he didn’t have enough fuel to attempt a getaway in the Toyota, Jessie frantically looked around to see a horse standing patiently off in the distance, down the backside of the hill from his position, as if waiting for his master to return. Realizing the horse must have belonged to the old man, Jessie knelt down beside him, placed his hand over his face, closed his eyes, and whispered softly, “I’m sorry.” Saying a silent prayer for the man, Jessie stood up and began a brisk walk down the backside of the hill toward the horse.

“Easy,” he said as he approached. “Good boy. Easy boy,” he repeatedly said as he took hold of the horse’s bridle. “Shhhh, shhh, it’s okay. I’m not gonna hurt you,” he whispered.

Placing one foot in the stirrup and swinging his other leg over the horse’s back, Jessie gently nudged him into action, and said, “Come on boy, let’s go,” as he rode down the north side of the hill and away from the rapidly approaching SUVs.

~~~~

Reaching the bottom of the hill, Jessie urged the horse down into a dried up, washed out gully that he assumed only held water after heavy rains. With brush growing alongside the gully, Jessie rode west, using it as visual cover. Reaching a point where he would be exposed to plain view, he brought the old horse to a stop, dismounted, and secured the horse's reins to a large rock, keeping him down in the wash and out of view from above.

Slipping his rifle through the brush, Jessie cupped his left hand over his scope’s objective lens in an attempt to shade it from the sun, reducing the chances of giving away his position
~~~~

with an inadvertent glint of light. After a few moments, he spotted movement on the hill above. At this range, he could make out a man in full SWAT-style gear, scanning the terrain below.

*Law enforcement?* Jessie wondered to himself. *Nah, can't risk it. Even if it is, that's liable to have been one of them's crazy uncle or something, and I'd have a hard time explaining why I had to shoot him.*

Checking the condition of his rifle, preparing to defend himself if necessary, Jessie verified that a round was in the chamber with the safety on. He gently placed the rifle on the ground next to him and drew his Colt, flipping open the loading gate and pushing the spent case out of the cylinder with the ejection rod, replacing it with a fresh round of .357 Magnum.

Returning the Colt to his holster, Jessie once again picked up his rifle and scanned the area above through his scope. *Nothing,* he thought. *Well, they're either gone or working their way around the hill to flank me.*

Resolved to the fact that he had better stay put for now, Jessie leaned back against a rock in the bottom of the dry wash, looked at the horse, and said, "As crazy as that man seemed, it looks like he managed to keep you fed. You help me get out of this, and I'll make sure that continues."

~~~~

For the next several hours, Jessie watched and listened patiently for signs of others. His mind drifting in and out of a guilt-driven depression brought on by the death of the man he'd had to shoot. *I couldn't have done anything differently,* he argued in his own mind. *He'd lost it. There was no reasoning with him. He was lost in the dark and twisted world his life had become, and there was no pulling him out of it in the few*
~~~~

*moments I had. If he would have happened across me right after Stephanie and the kids were taken, he'd have likely had to kill me, too. Damn it, though, I still could have, or should have, done something differently... but what?*

As darkness fell, Jessie looked at the horse and said, "I believe they're gone," as he stood and carefully looked around. Taking the horse's reins with his left hand, he rubbed the animal's neck with his right hand and said, "Come on boy. Let's take it slow and easy. Common sense tells me to head to the east away from this place, but my gut keeps telling me there's something I need to see in town." Chuckling to himself, he said, "If I keep listening to my gut, it's gonna be the end of me one of these days... but sometimes, I think that would be a gift."

Shaking himself out of the profoundly dark place that he had let his mind wander to, Jessie silently urged the horse forward, into the darkness and into the unknown.

## Chapter Seven

Her head pounding and her ears ringing, Leina woke to the horrible realization that the children were not with her. "Kayla! Gavin! Patricia!" she shouted, causing her to wince in pain. Putting her hand on the back of her head, Leina felt a bandage that was soaked in dried blood. Looking around the darkened room, lit only by the light shining underneath the door, she attempted to stand, only to immediately lie back down on the blanket strewn across the cold, concrete floor.

She felt as if she needed to vomit. The room was spinning; her thoughts were in disarray. *Where are my clothes?* she thought as she realized she was covered only with a thin bedsheet. She could hear the sounds of muffled voices coming from the next room, but could not understand the words.

*Something's not right,* she thought as the room spun around her. *What have they done to me? Where are my clothes? Where are the children? How did this happen? Earlier today, we were traveling with our friends, and now they're all dead. They died right in front of me. And the kids, oh, God, where are the children?* she thought as tears rolled down her cheek.

Her thoughts were suddenly interrupted as the door swung open, allowing the bright light of the adjacent room to shine inside. Holding her arm in front of her face while her eyes adjusted to the brightness, she heard a dark and familiar voice say, "What are you yelling about? What's going on in here?"

"Where are the children?" she asked frantically. "What have you done with them?"

"We've not done anything with them. They're being well cared for."

Fighting back her tears, Leina sobbed, "Where are they? Where's my baby girl? Where are Gavin and Patricia?"

Flipping on the lights in the room, the man began walking toward her. Leina recognized him as the one they had called Barnes. Another strange man, dressed in the same tactical attire, stood along behind him.

As he walked across the room, he held his finger to his lips and said, "Okay, calm down. There's no reason to get excited."

As he approached her, Leina shouted, "Get off me! Get away from me!"

Just then, a thundering voice shouted, "Barnes!"

Freezing in his tracks, Barnes turned to see the one they called "Chief" walking toward him with his hand on his holstered pistol. Shoving Barnes against the wall, staring at him directly in the eyes, the six-foot-tall, two-hundred-pound bruiser with a thick brown mustache and a shaved head said through gritted teeth, "What the hell is going on in here?"

"Nothing, Chief. I was just trying to calm her down. She was in here yelling and screaming."

"She had every right to be. What the hell do you think is going through her mind right now after what happened to her out there? Now, get out to the main gate and relieve Caldwell. He's been out there all day."

Without muttering a word, Barnes sheepishly scurried out of the room and down the hall.

The Chief then turned to the other man in the room and said, "Get her another dose. More this time," as he turned and began to walk out of the room.

"Yes, Chief," the man answered smartly as he turned toward Leina.

~~~~
~~~~

Beginning to awaken once again, her arms felt heavy as she tried to move. Lifting her head off the floor, she struggled to focus her vision, but everything looked blurry and distorted.

Startled by a voice, Leina struggled to slide against the wall behind her, her eyes beginning to regain their focus as the figure of a man slowly came into view.

Kneeling down in front of Leina, the one called Chief said, “Hello, ma’am. I'm sorry about all of this. This has been one hell of a rough day for you. You’ve got to have a thousand questions. First off, let me introduce myself. My name is Ken Perrone. I’m the Chief of Police here in Fort Sumner.”

Reacting with anger and rage, Leina shouted, “How could the police murder my friends and steal my children? How could you do that, you son-of-a-b—? Where are they? Give me my kids back!”

“Shhhhh, calm down,” he replied. “The children are fine. Several of our officers shuttled them across town to our medical clinic to have them checked out. They were pretty traumatized by what happened to your group earlier this evening. We are all saddened by your loss and are here to help. You see, you and your companions were ambushed by a group of bandits who owe an enormous debt to the drug cartels. After the collapse and the loss of value in paper currency, the cartels had to shift to operating with physical assets instead of cash. Fuel, weapons, and dare I say it, women and children, are their currency now. The bandits ambushed your group to take you and everything you had to pay their debts. We showed up just in the nick of time and ran them off.”

“That's not how I remember it,” she said defiantly, her head pounding as she struggled to maintain her focus.

“Well, you've been through a lot, and you took a pretty hard hit to the head during the crash. You're not remembering things clearly. You need your rest to get your head on straight.”

"Crash? What crash? We were attacked! You and your men attacked us! You killed my friends!"

"Ma'am, I'm sorry, but as I explained, we arrived on scene to find you and your group pinned down by bandits. Outside of our well-protected borders here in Fort Sumner, things like that seem to be happening more and more. They know people are trying to reach us for the safety our town provides, and they prey on that. We found you in an overturned minivan. The children were still in the vehicle with you. We struggled, but managed to get them pulled to safety through one of the windows. You must have hit your head during the rollover."

"What? But... That's not what happened. We were attacked."

"Yes, you were. That's what caused the crash. The driver of the van must have been shot, and the vehicle swerved and began to roll."

"No... That's not what happened. That's not..." Breaking down into tears, Leina was scared and confused. "Where are my clothes? Why am I naked?" she shouted as she held her sheet tightly around her body.

"I apologize for that, ma'am. Our staff EMT had to give you an examination to make sure you didn't suffer any injuries that weren't obvious to us. Don't worry, there were witnesses in the room. Your clothes are being laundered and will be returned to you soon—fresh and clean."

Interrupting before she could respond, another man entered the room, saying, "Chief, we've got reports of gunshots just outside of town."

"On my way," he replied. Chief Perrone turned back to Leina and said, "I've got to go. Duty calls. We'll continue this conversation after you're all rested up." Looking back at the other man in the room, he said, "Officer Reyes, get this young lady some adequate bedding. Make sure she gets some nice fluffy pillows, and for God's sake, get her some food and something to drink. Oh, and something for her pain."

"Yes, Chief," Reyes replied as he quickly turned and left the room.

"Well, miss... Uh, what's your name again?" Chief Perrone asked.

Pausing for a moment, her head spinning and the room becoming a blur, she reluctantly replied, "Leina. Well, my name is actually Leina'ala. It's Hawaiian, but I go by Leina to make it easy."

"It's nice to properly meet you, Leina'ala," he said with a warm smile. "We'll talk more in the morning when you're well rested, and your thoughts are clear. And don't worry, we'll get the children back to you as soon as the Doc signs off on them."

"Thank you," she replied as he quickly exited the room, pulling the door shut behind him.

Laying her head down on the blanket, her memories swirling around in her clouded mind, she fought the confusion that pervaded her thoughts. *Am I remembering things correctly?* she thought, questioning the validity of her own recollections. Her head throbbing in pain, she closed her eyes and longed for the luxury of sleep while she pictured the wonderful moment when Kayla, Gavin, and Patricia would be returned to her.

~~~~

Awakened by a knock, Leina looked up to see the door being slowly opened, once again casting light into the room. "Who's there?" she asked as her sleepy eyes attempted to focus on the figure standing in the doorway, shadowed by the bright lights.

"It's just me, ma'am. Officer Reyes. The chief had asked me to get you some proper bedding and something to eat."
~~~~

"Where are the children? Are they back?"

"They're staying at the clinic for the night where they can be kept safe. We had a murder just outside of town earlier. An elderly man, a lifelong resident of the area, was gunned down just a half-mile from our front gates. With the shooter still on the loose, Chief Perrone felt the safest course of action would be to wait until tomorrow to bring them back in the daylight. There are a lot of bad people out there. We do a good job of keeping them out of town, but they slip in from time to time. Considering that, the Chief doesn't want to take any unnecessary risks with the children."

Disappointed by his answer, Leina simply nodded in reply.

"This will make you more comfortable," he said as he reached outside the door, retrieving a folding cot from the hallway. Unfolding it and locking the legs into place, he said, "This will keep you off that cold, hard floor. I've got a few extra blankets and pillows for you as well."

Interrupted by another knock on the door, an elderly woman of Hispanic decent entered the room with a tray of food atop Leina's neatly folded and freshly laundered clothes. "Ah, Rosa is here with your dinner, if you're hungry, that is." Turning to Rosa, he politely said, "Thank you, ma'am. You can place the tray over there on the table."

"You're welcome, señor," she answered with a bow before quickly exiting the room.

Turning back to Leina, Officer Reyes said with a smile, "She's not much for conversation, but she's a true sweetheart. We'd be lost without her."

Still in a state of confusion, Leina started to speak, but found herself at a loss for words. "I... I... I don't..."

"It's okay. Like the Chief said, you've had a rough day," Reyes said as he shook two pills out of a medicine bottle retrieved from his pocket. "This will help with your pain."

"What... what is it?" she asked, sheepishly holding out her hand.

"We call it Vitamin M," he said with a chuckle. "It's Motrin, or Ibuprofen actually. Our doc gives it out like candy, no matter what our complaint is, so we just consider it our daily vitamin."

Seeing that she wasn't amused, he placed the pills into her hand and said, "Well, I'll let you get back to sleep. Sorry to wake you. If you need anything, just yell, and one of us will come running."

Looking around the room, noticing there were no windows on any of the walls, she asked, "What time is it?"

With a smile, he replied, "It's late. You should get some sleep. Someone will be by to check on you in the morning."

As he left the room, pulling the door shut behind him, Leina heard what sounded like a dead-bolt lock being engaged. Quickly reaching for her clothes while she was alone, Leina pulled her gray, long-sleeved T-shirt over her head, wrestled on her well-worn and faded blue jeans with a rip in the knee, and slid back underneath the covers before anyone returned.

She rolled over onto the cot, pulled the blankets around her tightly, and said to herself, "What the hell is going on here? I feel like I'm losing it. I can't even trust my own memories anymore," as she felt herself drifting once again into the darkness of unconsciousness.

## Chapter Eight

After an hour of walking the horse by the reins through the darkness of the night with only the moon to guide his way, Jessie's thoughts raced through his mind, his memories of the past colliding with thoughts of his present and his potential future. Snapping himself out of his downward mental spiral, Jessie looked at the old horse and said, "So, what's your name, anyway?"

After an awkward moment of silence, Jessie added, "Not much for words, I see. Well, if you're not gonna tell me, I'll just name you myself. Hmmm," he thought as he rubbed his chin and scrunched his forehead. "Eli. You look like an Eli. That's it. You're Eli now, old boy," patting him on the neck and tugging on his reins to get him moving again.

Feeling resistance from the tired, old horse, Jessie looked around and said, "Yeah, I'm tired, too. Let's find a place to bed down until sunrise. Heck, I don't even know for sure where I am. Once the sun is up, we'll get a good look at things, and I'll bounce what we see off the map, and we'll go from there. It looks like the terrain is getting a little more varied the further west we go. We'll find a safe spot soon."

~~~~

Feeling warmth on his face, Jessie felt a droplet of thick, warm liquid drip onto his chin. Opening his eyes, he was startled to see a large Rottweiler standing over him, its breath wreaking of rancid meat, drool hanging from its chin. Staring deeply into his eyes, the dog released a low, ominous growl.

Slowly moving his right hand toward his Colt revolver on his side, the dog, triggered by Jessie's movement, latched onto
~~~~

Jessie's arm with a bone-crushing bite while shaking its head back and forth violently.

Feeling the bones in his arm crack under the crushing force of the dog's vise-like grip, Jessie reached for his knife with his left hand and began stabbing the dog repeatedly, while screaming, "Get off me! Get off me! Get off me, you filthy beast!"

Striking the dog over and over again with the knife, the animal acted as if it wasn't fazed at all by Jessie's counterattack. Hearing sounds of struggle to his left, Jessie glanced over to see several other dogs dragging Eli to the ground. Leaping onto him like a pack of hungry lions, the dogs began to tear into the flesh of the old horse.

Releasing its mighty grip on Jessie's now severely lacerated and possibly broken arm, the dog looked into Jessie's eyes with a calculated stare. Hearing a whistle in the distance, the dog's head snapped to its left, in the direction of the sound, and immediately ran off with the rest of the pack in tow.

His arm in severe pain, Jessie's heart pounded as he looked around for any remaining threats, only to see Eli take his last gasp of air as he bled out, laying still and lifeless on the dry, dusty ground.

Hearing the low roar of a piston-driven, low-flying aircraft, Jessie was startled awake. Immediately grabbing his right arm, realizing it was okay, and it had all been yet another hellish nightmare, Jessie looked to see that Eli was unharmed as well, although he, too, was startled by the plane and was pulling nervously at his reins. Luckily, Jessie had secured Eli's reins to a large rock in the outcrop they had used for cover for the night, and the horse remained secure.

"Damn it!" Jessie exclaimed, his heart pounding in his chest. Grabbing his rifle, Jessie looked through the scope, zooming in on the aircraft. "That's a Beechcraft Baron," he murmured as he attempted to get as much information about his surroundings as he could in the pre-dawn light.

"That thing just took off," he said aloud in Eli's direction. "What the...?" Laying his rifle to the side while he pulled a well-worn, folded paper map out of his cargo pocket, Jessie scanned the map for the Red Lake and Fort Sumner area, trying to get his bearings on where exactly he might be. Tracing the map with his finger, Jessie said, "Fort Sumner Municipal Airport. We've got to be right here," tapping his finger on the map.

Shoving the map back into his pocket, Jessie retrieved his rifle once again and began tracking the aircraft as it headed south, over the horizon, and out of sight. *Where the heck are they going?* he wondered.

With the airplane fully out of sight, Jessie retrieved his map and began to study his potential situation. *If this is the airport, then the town is directly south of us over that slight rise in the terrain. Maybe I can go get a look-see.*

Putting the map back into his pocket, Jessie turned to Eli and said, "Eli, old boy, I'm gonna need you to stay put for a bit. I need to work my way to that hilltop to see if I have my bearings straight. I need to keep a low profile, so I'll just leave you here for now, but don't worry, I'll be back."

Gathering his pack and rifle, Jessie turned and looked at Eli and thought, "Ah hell, I can't leave him here without breakfast." Placing his pack and rifle back on the ground, Jessie walked around the immediate vicinity, pulling any sort of forage from its roots that he thought Eli might like. With a small armload of grasses and legumes, Jessie placed them in front of the horse, who immediately began pushing it around with his nose, sifting through the pile for the most desirable choices.

"Picky ol' boy, ain't you?" he said, patting him on the back. "You'd think a horse as skinny as you would just be happy to have a meal."

Jessie then removed a water bottle from his pack and poured its contents into his own campfire cooking pan for Eli to drink. "There you go, buddy. Now, hang tight. I'll be back."

Once again donning his pack and shouldering his rifle, Jessie worked his way cautiously toward the rising terrain in the distance, due south of his position. As he neared the highest point of the terrain, devoid of any trees or adequate vegetation that could be used as cover while he observed what lay down below, Jessie slipped off his pack and placed it to the side. Slinging his rifle over his back, he then crawled on all fours to the summit, and slowly peeked over the edge. *There she is,* he thought as he observed the town below. *Fort Sumner.*

Lying on his stomach, Jessie pulled his rifle around, shouldering it to use the scope to aid him in getting a better look off in the distance below. Cupping his hand over the scope's objective lens in an attempt to avoid any unwanted glints of light, Jessie scanned slowly and methodically, looking for signs of movement.

Panning from left to right, Jessie saw a man and a small child walking down one of the side streets, carrying a few small bags. *Hmm,* he thought. *Is this town still alive? Did it not get hit?*

Just then, an SUV painted in a makeshift desert/plains-style camo paint job entered his field of view from the left. The SUV had the telltale signs of being a current or former law enforcement vehicle of some sort, with a push-style brush guard on the front, an A-pillar-mounted spotlight and a light bar on top. Any pre-existing agency markings had long since been painted over, though. *Who the hell is that?* he thought.

Watching the vehicle that was now just one street over from the adult and child, Jessie noticed the adult pull the child by the arm, ducking behind a fence and a decorative hedgerow. *What the...?*

The SUV slowly worked its way down the street, passing by the people hidden behind the fence without incident. *Now, just why did those people not want to interact with you, boys?* he thought as the vehicle slowly worked its way through town as if on a patrol.

Once the vehicle was well past the hidden adult and child, the two emerged onto the street once again, where they hurried to a home just several houses down. *At a glance, this looks like suburbia, but things seem a bit tense.*

Off to his right, Jessie could see another SUV kicking up a trail of dust off in the distance, traveling from the north to the south, approaching the northern edge of town. Turning his attention to this second vehicle, Jessie thought, *he looks like he's traveling from roughly where the airport is located. Hmmm... Was he associated with that departing aircraft? I guess I'll have to take a closer look.*

## Chapter Nine

"Rise and shine," Leina heard a man's voice say as she opened her eyes and felt the room begin to spin.

"What...huh?" she murmured as she tried to focus.

"It's okay," the man said. "It's me, Chief Peronne. Did my men take good care of you last night?"

"I don't...I don't really remember. I...I don't remember much of anything. It's all a blur. The kids! Where are the kids?" she said as the fog in her mind began to clear.

Taking a seat next to her on the cot, he placed his hand on hers and said, "They're safe and sound, but we still haven't found the assailant that killed one of our townspeople. We've had reports from residents that he's inside our town's perimeter. With that in mind, we feel it prudent to keep the kids on lockdown at the clinic. We have several of our officers on scene there twenty-four hours a day, so they will be safe."

"Can't your men there just bring them here?" she asked, feeling panic begin to set in. "I need to see my children. They need me. You can't keep them away from me like this."

"Ma'am. Like I said, we're making every effort to ensure the safety and the well-being of the children. Hopefully, we'll come to a resolution soon in our attempts to capture the perpetrator. That has to be our first priority, though. If we take our officers away from the clinic to escort the children, and then something happens at the clinic, well, you can see where that just wouldn't be in the town's best interests. The feeling of security is a fragile thing these days. To be honest, making sure nothing happens to anyone inside our borders isn't just about the safety and well-being of the individuals involved; it's about the psyche of everyone else. Our people feel safe here. They've all been through hell, though. Before we got a grip on things, that is.

That feeling of security would be lost if anything happened inside of our safe zone. So, I don't mean to sound rude, but it's not just about the safety of you and your children. It's about the peace of mind of our citizens as well. We can't let anything at all happen that would compromise the security that our residents feel."

Piecing his words together in her mind, she asked, "Town? You have a functioning town?"

"Yes, ma'am," Chief Perrone replied. "We have a clinic. We have a community garden. We have a school for the children. We have—"

"You have a school?" she interrupted.

"Why, yes. Well, it's more of a one-room school, like in the old days. A few of the teachers from the elementary school, from before the attacks, have remained in town and do a pretty good job keeping our kids up to speed in their studies. We will need to expand things in the long run, but for now, it works just fine."

"So, you're the chief of police here?"

"Yes, ma'am," he replied confidently.

"Have you always been the chief? You know, since before?"

"I've been with the Fort Sumner Police Department since before it all began."

"As the chief?" she quickly asked again.

"Well, before the attacks and the fighting started, I was a lieutenant. A few months into the collapse, the previous chief was killed in the line of duty, and I was next in the chain of succession."

Pausing for a moment to digest what he said, she then asked, "Is the mayor still in town?"

"No, he didn't make it either."

"What happened to him?"

"A lot of bad things happened. I can't document them all for you right now. The mayor was merely one of many who got caught up in the ensuing violence of it all."

"So, who is in charge? Ultimately, that is, for the town?"

With a perturbed look on his face, Chief Peronne stood up and replied, "I am." Looking at his watch, he said, "Well, I hope you feel better today than you did yesterday. You have sure been through a lot. I've got to get going. I just wanted to stop by and see how you were doing. If you need anything at all, don't hesitate to ask the officer who's just outside the door."

"Am I confined here?" she asked inquisitively.

"Confined? No. But we are on lockdown pending the apprehension of the assailant. Like I said, we take security very seriously here. So for now, it would be best if you just stay put where we can keep you safe."

Turning to leave the room, Chief Peronne paused and turned back to Leina, saying in a calm and reassuring voice, "I know this is a lot to take in. I know you lost some of your friends back there, and you're still worried about the kids. Anyone would be full of worry and doubt in this situation. But trust me, you're safe, the kids are safe, and it's all going to be just fine from here on out. This is a real, functioning town full of wonderful people. Once we catch the murderer, you'll be reunited with the children, and you'll start to see that for yourself. We've been through a lot too, just like you. We've lost a lot of our own, including the mayor, as I mentioned, to the violence of the world outside our gates. That's why we take situations like this so seriously. We've learned the hard way that in order to ensure the safety of our residents, we have to take immediate action and not relent until each and every security situation is resolved. It won't be much longer, I promise. But you have to respect that."

Answering only with a nod and a look of understanding, Leina watched as Chief Peronne turned and left the room, pulling the door shut and locking it once again from the outside.

## Chapter Ten

Slipping into a position of cover on the northwest edge of town, Jessie watched as the sun disappeared over the horizon, casting a shadow of the coming night over the town of Fort Sumner. Nestled behind the post of an advertising billboard, on a small hill surrounded by wild brush, Jessie peered through his scope, being careful not to allow the sun's final rays to reflect directly off his lens. *Only a few more minutes of useful light,* he thought. *Spence should have stolen me a night-vision scope if he was gonna go through the hassle,* he thought to himself with a chuckle as he fondly thought of his friends Spence, Jörgen and the others that he had left behind.

Returning his thoughts to the task at hand, Jessie scanned the town looking for signs of movement. Seeing the back door of a small, one-story ranch-style home open halfway, Jessie paused his scan and focused on the movement. Seeing a young woman's head appear from the doorway, seeming to scan the area as if she was looking for potential threats, he observed as she slipped from the door, hurrying across the back yard of the home with what appeared to him to be a laundry basket full of freshly folded clothes. As she reached the neighboring house, its back door seemed to be opened from within as the young woman hurried inside.

"Everyone sure seems to be on edge around here," he whispered to himself, turning his attention elsewhere.

Seeing one of the camo-painted SUV's slowly work its way down the street from the east to the west, Jessie noticed as it stopped periodically at each intersecting side street. As the failing light of the sun finally gave way to darkness, Jessie sat his rifle aside and continued to watch the vehicle as it now began using an A-pillar mounted spotlight to scan its surroundings, slowing working its way through town.

Looking up at the clear night sky, Jessie reassessed his position in relation to the bright moonlight being cast down upon him. Being in the shadow of the billboard above, he thought, *I'm still good here.* Chuckling under his breath as he gazed up at the billboard above, Jessie couldn't help but laugh at the picture of a cow trying to talk fast-food patrons into eating chicken instead of beef. *That's what did us in,* he thought. *Everyone was okay with whatever was going on in the country and in the world as long as it was someone else's rights being trampled, and not theirs. The problem with that flawed logic is that the attention will eventually be on you, and then, there will no one else willing to help, either. We were the cows and the chickens. If only our proverbial cows and chickens could have understood the strength they would have had if they would have simply stood together, and didn't just watch silently as the others were being taken off to slaughter by the farmer.*

~~~~

After several hours of still calm, interrupted intermittently by the passing of a patrolling vehicle in the town below, Jessie watched as a vehicle approached a home on the north edge of town. Unlike before, this time, the men in the vehicle, all dressed and equipped the same as the others, exited the SUV and moved to form a perimeter around the home as two of the men approached the front of the house. Spotlights from the vehicle illuminated the area, allowing Jessie to see.

Unable to hear what was going on due to the distance to the home, Jessie carefully watched and observed, taking special note of the behavior and mannerisms of the men. *They move like a*
~~~~

*well-trained unit,* he thought, noting their textbook movements and procedures.

After repeated attempts to get the occupants of the house to answer the door, Jessie watched as the men kicked the door from its hinges, quickly entering the home, weapons drawn, one aiming high and one aiming low. After a few moments, the men who had forcefully entered the home reemerged, one carrying what appeared to be a young woman, kicking and screaming, while the other beat back an elderly man with the butt of his rifle, finally taking the man to the ground.

Forcing the young woman into the vehicle, the men sped away, turning east toward the direction from which they came. The elderly man, now lying motionless on the ground in front of the home, was quickly retrieved by several other occupants of the home, and taken inside.

"What the hell?" Jessie mumbled to himself, unable to know for sure what had just taken place before his very eyes.

~~~~

Remaining silently in position for what felt like several more hours, Jessie checked the time on his watch and looked up at the moon in the sky. *It's almost three in the morning,* Jessie thought. *I'd better fall back, get back to Eli, and get some sleep. Who knows what tomorrow will bring.*

As he lowered his head and turned to look back toward Fort Sumner below, Jessie caught movement out of the corner of his eye off to his left flank. Quickly picking up his rifle, he focused as best he could with what little light he had. Rotating the rifle at an angle, avoiding the scope, he looked through the forty-five-degree offset iron sights mounted on his rifle in an attempt to once again catch movement in his peripheral vision while being ready to engage a threat.
~~~~

*There!* he thought as he saw the form of a man moving past his left flank, heading in a direction away from the town and into the darkness. Quickly realizing that where there is one, there is likely more, Jessie felt that his position had been most certainly compromised. Undoubtedly, there would be another threat ahead of him, as well as off to his right flank, and given enough time for them to get into position, he would be boxed in from behind as well. *Not tonight, boys,* he thought as he slipped away from the billboard, moving as low and stealthily as he could, falling back, away from the town.

Working his way through the dry, arid landscape, attempting to use the natural lay of the terrain to hide in the shadows of the moonlight as best he could, Jessie heard movement from the darkness ahead as a voice quietly said, "Drop your weapon."

Without taking another step, his rifle already trained on the source of the sound, Jessie saw a figure emerge from the shadows before him. A man in his early thirties, dressed in the same law enforcement style tactical gear as the others he had seen, held aim on him with an M4-style patrol carbine pointed directly at his chest.

"I said drop your weapon," the man once again quietly insisted.

In a calm and steady voice, Jessie replied, "This rifle has a two-and-a-half-pound match-grade competition trigger. I'm already applying about a pound or a pound and a half of force. If you shoot, or if one of your buddies hiding off in the darkness shoots, the slightest twitch of my body as it takes the bullet will send a .308 round into your chest. At this close range, that vest won't do anything for you," Jessie said, referring to the man's protective vest worn underneath his load-bearing web-gear. "You don't have the position of authority here, son. You think you're giving me an order, but to me, you're simply offering to trade me one of your puny little 5.56 rounds for my .308. I'll take that trade. Are you willing to accept my counter-offer?"

Looking around nervously, the man said, "Look, just lower your rifle and I'll just walk away."

With a chuckle, Jessie replied, "I'm not new to the art of negotiating at gunpoint. I've been doing it for years. I'm also not ignorant of the manual of arms in regards to your little rifle there. You're a rookie, aren't you?" Jessie asked in a dismissive tone.

"What?" the man nervously asked.

"If you so much as twitch, I'll smoke you," Jessie said. "Keep your thumb exactly where it is. You see, only a rookie would have brought his M4 to bear with the safety engaged. Before you are able to click that off with your thumb, I'll have added that one extra pound of force I need to this trigger. The most that fancy ballistic vest will do for you at this range is to catch my bullet as it comes out of your back. It may do a good job of containing the splatter, but that's about it."

With a look of fear in the man's eyes, Jessie continued. "Now that we're both clear on exactly where we stand, call your friends out and tell them to drop their weapons."

"I can't do that," the man said.

"Then I guess our trade is on," Jessie replied in a calm and callous voice.

"N...no," the man stammered. "I'm alone."

"Bull," Jessie replied insistently. "They wouldn't have sent you out here alone. Now call them out or I'll call them out with the crack of my rifle as it smokes you."

"I'm alone. I swear. Okay, okay, I'm putting my rifle down," the man said as his finger came off the trigger and he slowly and carefully removed the weapon's sling from around his neck and lowered it to the ground.

Motioning with the barrel of his rifle, Jessie then said, "Now, the nine millimeter. Drop it, too."

Complying with Jessie's demands, the man took a few steps back from the pistol as Jessie snarled, "I didn't tell you to move."

Jessie then began slowly working his way forward, and through gritted teeth, said, "I said call them out."

"Sir, I told you. I'm alone."

"Bull..." Jessie said. "I hate a liar."

Seeing the rage in Jessie's eyes, the man pleaded, "I swear, I'm telling you the truth. I came out here alone. I was just..." and before he could finish, the man was interrupted by the sight of the butt of Jessie's AR10 rifle, sending him into a world of total darkness.

## Chapter Eleven

Pacing back and forth across the room, Leina anxiously awaited the arrival of the children as Chief Peronne had promised. The lack of windows in the room had led to her completely losing track of time. Not even sure of the time of day, her thoughts raced uncontrollably through her mind about when she might be reunited once again with the children.

Hearing a gentle knock on the door, Leina's heart raced with anticipation as her voice trembled, saying, "Yes, come in," as she began to walk toward the door. Disappointed to see a lone officer enter the room, with no sign of the children, she frantically asked, "Are they here? The kids... where are they?"

"Good evening, ma'am," the young, clean-cut man in his late twenties said as he removed his uniform hat, placing it underneath his left arm.

Leina couldn't help but notice that he was carrying a gift bag with rope-style handles in his left hand.

"Chief Peronne asked me to bring you to his quarters so that he can catch you up on everything. He thought you might need a break from this room, so he sent two of us to escort you safely to his home. My name is Fox, Officer Scott Fox. My partner, in the vehicle outside, is Officer Gabriel Fernandez. We will see to it that you get there safe and sound, and then Chief Peronne can answer any questions that you may have." Awkwardly pausing, he continued, "Oh, here you go. Chief Peronne thought you might also want to get into a clean set of clothes. A lady needs more than just one outfit," he said with a smile.

Reluctantly reaching for the bag, she asked, "What's this?" as she opened it, revealing its contents.

"Just a little something to help you get cleaned up a bit. I'll be waiting outside the door while you change. No rush, ma'am."

Leina watched as he left the room, pulling the door shut behind him. She then removed the clothing from the bag to find a satin, sleeveless dress. *I don't think so,* she thought as she tossed it on her cot.

Opening the door slowly and walking out of the room, Leina saw Officer Fox with his back against the wall and one foot propped up on the wall behind him. Quickly gathering himself, as she'd caught him off guard, she could see that he was surprised that she hadn't changed into the dress he had provided for her. "It wasn't my style," she said sharply.

"Not a problem, ma'am. We were just trying to help. Anyway, if you will come with me, we will get on our way so that the chief can answer any questions you may have.

~~~~

As they drove a short distance from the building where she had been kept since her arrival, Leina thought to herself about how quaint of a little town this must have been before it all began to fall apart—as well as how well it had been kept up, for that matter. Most places she had seen along the way were in shambles from fighting and neglect. This place, however, would almost look normal if not for the lack of people out and about.

"The chief's house is just up ahead," Officer Fox said from the front passenger seat, interrupting her thoughts. "For security reasons, Officer Fernandez here will stay with the vehicle and keep it running while I escort you to the front door. Once inside, you will be safe. Chief Peronne has armed guards at his place twenty-four-seven. He'll radio us when you are ready to leave, and we will be back to get you."

Only nodding in reply, Leina's heart raced in anticipation of what this meeting might bring. *Oh please, God, let the children*
~~~~

*be here. I miss my babies,* she thought as a tear ran down her cheek. *Please let this nightmare come to an end.*

As the vehicle slowly came to a stop in front of a large, white house that appeared far beyond the financial means of a municipal police chief, Officer Fernandez made an abrupt radio call in a muffled voice, followed by an equally muted response, and said to Officer Fox, "Good to go."

"Roger that," Fox responded. Turning to Leina in the back seat, he said, "Here we are. I'll escort you inside. Just sit tight and wait until I open your door from the outside," he said as he began to exit the vehicle.

Leina scanned the area around the house. The thick, lush hedges in front of the home had clearly been meticulously maintained and watered. The sharp, squared-off, decoratively-shaped bushes were surrounded by a well-kept and recently mowed lawn that seemed to have been cared for with great attention to detail. From her vantage point, she could see what appeared to be a pool house behind the home, adorned with the same elaborate window treatments and large white columns as the entryway at the main house. Her thoughts quickly shifted to the situation at hand, as her door was opened abruptly from the outside by Officer Fox.

"Ma'am," he said, motioning for her to exit the vehicle.

Slipping out without saying a word, Leina followed Officer Fox up the decorative stone walkway leading to the front door of the home. As they approached the front door, it opened from the inside as a large, muscular man nodded to Fox, saying, "The chief is in his study. You can take her on back."

Turning to Leina, Officer Fox said, "Right this way," as he shared a grin with the large man at the door. The man nodded as they passed, the door closing firmly behind them with the sliding deadbolt being immediately placed into the lock position.

Following Officer Fox through the home, Leina found the interior of the home to be equally as lavish and well cared for. As they approached a set of large, wooden double-doors, her heart raced as she listened for any sounds of children. To her dismay, all she could hear was the faint sound of jazz music emanating from the room.

Stopping just shy of the door, Officer Fox knocked, followed by the sound of footsteps approaching the door from within the room. As the door slowly opened, Leina could see that it was Chief Peronne, dressed in pleated gray slacks and a French-cuffed white dress shirt with a black leather belt and matching wing tip, Oxford-style dress shoes.

"Ah, Miss Sallander, it's so nice to see you up and about," Chief Peronne said with a smile on his face as he reached out to take her hand, leading her into the room. "That'll be all, for now, Fox," he then said while closing the door, leaving Leina alone with him in the room.

Walking over to an old antique record player, Chief Peronne lowered the volume and said, "I'm sorry. That was a bit loud. I love jazz. I just can't get enough. There's something about the controlled chaos of it all. Jazz music didn't stay within the boundaries of what society had previously defined."

Removing the cork from a bottle of wine, filling two glasses as he spoke, he continued, "The early jazz musicians did things their own way. They didn't follow a traditional meter, beat, or formal structure. They improvised, doing what they had to do, moving the song along. I admire that," he said as he seemed to get lost for a moment in the music with his eyes closed, swaying his head to the rhythm.

Turning to her and looking her over, he said, "Did you not like the dress?"

"Mrs.," she said abruptly.

"I'm sorry, what?"

"It's Mrs. Sallander, not Miss," she replied sharply.

As the sparkle faded slightly from his smile, Chief Peronne replied, "Oh, I'm sorry. You hadn't mentioned a husband, only the children. I guess I thought you were single. My mistake."

Pausing for a moment, Leina said, "My husband, Cas, was killed by a group that tried to rob us several months after the collapse began."

"I'm sorry to hear that," Peronne replied in a softened tone.

"Don't be," she said. "He went down swinging. He almost took out the entire mob before one of them stabbed him in the back while he fought off two others from the front. I've never seen a man fight so hard. I've never seen such absolute power and ferocity in a human being. Most women I know would remember that scene as a horrific tragedy. Me, I remember it as the moment I realized no man will ever be able to live up to him. He's my forever—even though he's no longer with us. His fight, his spirit, it's what's kept me going all this time."

After an awkward pause, Chief Peronne replied, "I admire that. Let's drink a toast to his memory," he said as he handed her a glass of red wine.

"He's not a memory," Leina replied. "He's a part of me."

The smile quickly extinguishing from his face, he turned and sat her glass of wine on the elegantly carved bar by the fireplace and said, "So... I've got a proposition for you."

"Where are the children?" she asked firmly.

"Oh, they are safe, and I want to ensure that they stay that way, which is why I have an offer for you."

"You want to ensure they stay that way? What the hell does that mean?"

"Hey, relax," he said. "I didn't mean that in a negative or threatening way. I'm sorry if it sounded that way. I was referring to their long-term safety. I simply want to give you and the children a future that ensures your security and well-being."

"I've done a pretty good job of ensuring their safety. Now where are they?" she insisted.

"Have you, now?" he responded in a condescending tone. "If my men hadn't rescued you when they did..."

"Rescued," she interrupted. "My memory is a little unclear, but the one thing I know deep in my heart is that your men didn't rush in and save the day. I'm not sure what's going on here, but if I don't get to see the kids soon..."

"Miss Sallander," he interrupted in an attempt to redirect the tension that was rapidly building in the room.

"Mrs. Sallander," she again firmly replied.

"Of course, my mistake, Mrs. Sallander," he said, correcting himself. "I didn't bring you here to get you all riled up and angry. The children will be returned to you this evening. Our officers are on a pretty tight schedule as we are spread thin with the extra patrols initiated by the security breach on the edge of town. I have several officers slated to escort them from the clinic at six o'clock."

"You had the manpower to escort me to your home, but you didn't have the manpower to bring the children to me?"

"It's complicated," he said, pausing to gather his thoughts. "There is a lot going on these days, to say the least. However, I think it is important that you hear what I have to say, so if you don't mind, I'd like to get on with it."

Crossing her arms in protest, she said, "Go ahead."

"What I was trying to say," he said as he finished his glass of wine, "was that our little community here is about as safe as it gets these days. We're basically still a fully functioning town, with all of the things people need not just to survive, but to thrive. We are missing a few things, though. We could use someone like you to help out in the school, or at city hall. Just because the world is falling apart around us, doesn't mean we can't adequately keep up with the administration of our town. If you are willing to stay, we can provide you with a home, with food, with medical care, and school for the children. You're just not going to find that level of security for yourself or the children anywhere else out there, I'm afraid. And if you insist on leaving with those kids, well, I'm just not sure I would feel comfortable letting you put them at risk out there on your own."

"Letting? What are you saying?"

"I just want you to know that you have options now. You don't have to be out there where who knows what will happen to you."

Attempting to process the myriad thoughts swirling around her head, Leina stared at the large, finely crafted bookshelf that spanned an entire wall in the room as she noticed him once again pick up her glass of wine, handing it to her, saying, "I apologize that this conversation got off on the wrong foot. Let's start over. Let's just relax and discuss what we have to offer you and the children while we wait for them to arrive."

Reaching out to take the glass against her own better judgment, Leina acquiesced, taking a seat on a leather chair next to the bookshelf. "I'm listening," she said, taking a sip of wine.

## Chapter Twelve

His head throbbing in pain, the man awoke to find himself face down on the back of a horse, his feet hanging off one side, his head and hands over the other. Struggling in a panic, the man soon realized that his hands and feet were bound together by a rope extending underneath the horse's abdomen. Unable to see due to the cloth bag over his head that was tied securely around his neck, the man's struggles did nothing but increase his pain, and to cause him once again to slip off into the dark and silent prison of unconsciousness.

~~~~

Being nearly drowned by a face full of water, the man coughed and gagged, trying to expel the fluid from his mouth, nose, and lungs. Regaining his composure, the man looked around the room to see that he was tied securely to a chair in the center of a room, illuminated only by a few rays of light that shone in through the gaps in the dusty, old curtains.

His head still throbbing with pain, the man closed his eyes momentarily to regroup, when he heard the gritty voice of the man he had encountered the night before.

"It's about time you woke up," Jessie said as he walked behind the man, slowly drawing his knife across a stone just as a butcher would sharpen his tools before processing a properly aged carcass. His boots causing the old, wooden floor to creak with each step.

Shaking his head to clear the water from his face, the man coughed again and said, "What... what the hell? Who are you?"

"I'm just a man looking for answers," Jessie replied as he stepped around into the man's view, his hat pulled down low
~~~~

with his head tilted down to obscure his face, slowly working the blade of his knife to perfection.

His eyes locked on the blade, the man nervously said, “What kind of answers?”

“Why were you out there in the dark? Were you looking for someone? Someone... like me?” Jessie asked.

“Who are you? I... I don’t know what you...”

“Stop the babbling and get to it!” Jessie shouted. “You wouldn’t have just been out for a stroll, enjoying the night sky with your patrol rifle, sidearm, a vest, and all of your gear. What were you looking for?”

“Look, if you’re with Márquez, I didn’t have anything to do with that. We loaded what the chief told us to load. I was just doing what I was instructed to do,” the man insisted. “Several of us told him it was a bad idea. He didn’t want to hear it. But I... I didn’t have any control over that.”

Pausing for a moment to contemplate the man’s sudden confession, Jessie said, “Yeah, well, you’re guilty of participating in whatever you go along with. No man can force you to do anything but die. A man can take your life. He can cut your throat while you’re hogtied to a chair and laugh as you bleed out. A man can have that kind of control over you very easily,” Jessie said as he reflected a glint of light from the windows with the blade of his knife. “But anything you do with your own hand, whether ordered to do so or of your own accord... you own that. Cowardice toward the man who pretends to wield power over you is not an excuse. You make the choice. You can stand up for what is right, even if it costs you your life, or you can choose to be a willing participant. Which, as you can clearly see right now, at this moment, can also cost you your life. That’s your call. No one can make you be a part of his wrongs without your consent.”

"That's why I'm out!" the man insisted. "I'm done. That's why I was out there in the dark. I was leaving. It's not me you want. It's them... or him, rather."

After a few moments of silence, contemplating his next move, Jessie said, "If you were leaving, where were you going?"

"I have... or had, family in northern Oklahoma," the man stated in a defeated tone as he gazed at the floor.

"Where in northern Oklahoma?" Jessie asked.

Looking Jessie in the eye, the man replied, "I'd be a fool to tell you that. I'd never lead you and your men back home. I'd rather you just go ahead and kill me now. It's bad enough that I didn't go back home to help defend the farm when this all started. It's bad enough that I stayed here as long as I have, getting deeper and deeper into the mess that I'm in, instead of being with my parents and my brothers and sisters during all of this. I'll be damned if I mess up again and tell you any more than I already have. Just do it," he said, hanging his head low and closing his eyes. "Just get it over with. I'm not going to tell you anything else."

Pacing across the room and gazing out of the crack in the curtains, Jessie said, "Fair enough. I won't ask you any more about where you are heading, but if you tell me about what you're running from, and what you've been a part of... and if I can verify that you're telling me the truth, I'll let you live. I'll let you continue your journey north to live out your days being eaten alive by guilt."

"You're not with Márquez, are you?" the man said, looking at Jessie with an inquisitive look on his face.

Turning back toward the man while pulling the curtains fully closed, Jessie said, "Like you, if what you say is true, I'm just a man trying to get to his family."

"Then why were you standing watch over Fort Sumner? Why didn't you just steer clear of the place? Or... or did you hear the radio transmissions?"

"Radio transmissions?" Jessie queried.

Breaking eye contact with Jessie, staring blankly across the room, the man explained, "The chief..."

"Chief?" Jessie interrupted.

"Yes, the chief of police, Chief Peronne. Anyway, the chief commandeered a local man's HAM radio setup to broadcast occasional messages that announced that Fort Sumner was a safe haven with food, water, and medical care. He would then set up ambushes on the main migration routes outside of town to steal from those seeking refuge. After that ruse had begun to bring results, he got the town's old AM radio station up and running and began transmitting at a low power setting on AM as well. He wanted to attract people, but not too many to be able to deal with."

"Why the hell would he do that?" Jessie snarled. "Let's back up. Start from the beginning. Tell me the whole story, starting with your name."

"My name is Toby Robertson. Most people call me T. R.," the man said as he began to explain. "When the attacks began, I was a hydraulics tech at a local heavy equipment shop. You know, dozers, loaders, graders, and such."

Nodding in reply, Jessie said, "Go on."

"When the attacks began, being a small town in the middle of the desert, we were sheltered from most of what was going on. We were small fish to the terrorists and their allies, I guess. But when the federal government abandoned the border and redirected the USBP personnel to protect political interests, the cartels south of the border, who we later found out were in cahoots with the Islamic extremists and everyone else who seemed to be in on it, seized the opportunity to rush in and take over. Sheriff Whitaker, the De Baca County Sheriff at the time, was killed in front of his home, beheaded, and impaled on his own flagpole to send a message to whoever would seek to replace him. The corpse and the blood-covered upside-down flag sent a pretty strong message at that."

Pausing for a moment to gather his thoughts and to shake off some of his more haunting memories, he continued, "The chief of police at the time, Chief Vasquez, was a good man. He and the mayor set up a defensive perimeter around the town and enlisted the help of many of the local able-bodied men to try and keep the cartels away. It was a pretty violent time, to say the least. Our guys were getting picked off and ambushed left and right. Then one night, both the mayor and Chief Vasquez were murdered, their homes burned, and their families taken."

"What became of their families?" Jessie asked.

"We don't have a clue. We never saw them again. That's when Lieutenant Peronne stepped up and declared himself the interim chief of police. He promised we would hold an election for a new mayor, who would then appoint a permanent chief of police as soon as things stabilized. To date, that simply hasn't happened."

In an inquisitive tone, Jessie asked, "The election hasn't happened, or things becoming stabilized hasn't happened?"

"The election. Well, both, really. As soon as Peronne took over, the cartels backed off, and things settled down. For about a month, things started to seem like they would be okay. I joined the Fort Sumner Municipal Police because, at the time, it not only seemed like the right thing to do, it was the only thing to do. The shop I worked at closed its doors, like most businesses, so I had nowhere else to turn. As a police officer, I would at least always have a roof over my head and food on my plate. It seemed like the only sure thing."

Pausing to collect his thoughts, T. R. continued, “It wasn’t long after that, though, that I began to realize why the cartels had backed off. It wasn’t because Peronne was doing such a good job of keeping us safe, it was because he and the cartels had an understanding of sorts. You see, with the collapse of paper currency, and electronic financial instruments as the nation and world around us spiraled out of control, the cartels found themselves in the same dilemma as everyone else. Money, unless it was precious metals, was simply no good. People wanted to trade real assets that they could use to survive. Food, fuel, supplies, guns, ammunition, all became the new money. And if you were on the wrong side of humanity, as many were, women and children, especially little girls, also became currency. They became like gold to the cartels. They became traffickers in the sex trade as well as the drug trade. The products that will always sell, not matter how screwed up the world gets, are sex and drugs.”

“So, the ambushes are used to acquire items to trade with the cartels?” Jessie asked as he began to see the big picture.

“Some of it was for the town. Some of it was for trade and payoffs,” T. R. replied. “The area around the town basically became a big spider web, and Peronne was the spider. But since he keeps the town on such a tight lockdown—for their own safety of course—the townspeople basically have no idea what’s going on outside their borders. Peronne then turned our local airport into a transportation hub for whatever the cartels wanted to move. He provided unimpeded access to the airport, as well as security for those coming and going while moving their goods. In return, the cartels left him alone and did not target him like they had his predecessors. They let him create a little kingdom for himself here in Fort Sumner, and he is always looking for ways to ensure his position by providing them with whatever material and physical support he can.”

"And the local citizens?" Jessie asked. "How do they fare in this new kingdom? From what I have seen, things seem a little tense."

"They fare about as well as the peasants of tyrant kings of the past, I guess. They are all forced to contribute in one way or another. Whether it's food production, labor, or entertainment for his men, everyone has to pay their fair share. Fair as he sees it, at least."

Turning away in disgust, Jessie attempted to retain his composure. Confused with how to handle his prisoner, who seemed like a man who was simply caught up in an unfortunate situation, Jessie paced back and forth anxiously. "How do I deal with you?" he asked. "You lent your services to a traitor who enslaved your fellow man. Don't give me that crap answer that you were just following orders, either."

Hanging his head low, T. R. took a deep breath, and replied, "I... I don't know. I'm not ashamed that I joined the police department. At the time, it was the right thing to do, or so I thought. But I am ashamed that I didn't leave when I realized how things were going down."

"Leave? Leave?" Jessie shouted. "You should have fought back, you coward! You should have taken a stand with your fellow man, not against your fellow man! There is no worse betrayal a man can do than to side against his neighbor and stand with tyranny. Over and over throughout history, tyrants have been empowered by cowards who either did nothing or just followed orders to make things easier for themselves. It's easy to do that. It's easy to follow orders and act as if you don't have a choice. It's hard to take a stand as a true patriot—to know that the first who stands up for freedom and what is right, will likely die. I would rather live a short life, having contributed to the freedom of those who follow me, than to live a long life feeling like a coward and a traitor."

Storming out of the house, slamming the door behind him in disgust, Jessie left T. R. to his thoughts. Tears streaming down his face, T. R was overcome with emotion as Jessie's words struck a massive blow to his heart.

Whispering through the tears, T. R. said, "Please, Lord, help me make this right."

## Chapter Thirteen

Jessie's thoughts raced through his mind. He thought of the vehicles he had found east of town, and how the scene was eerily reminiscent of the scenario painted by T. R. Had the people who were ambushed on the road been lured into a trap set by Peronne? Were there children in the minivan, as it had appeared? Where are they now? All of those questions begged to be answered. The only thing Jessie was certain of was that he couldn't live with himself if he simply moved on and let other unsuspecting travelers face the same fate. Desperation in this wretched new world would lead others to follow such false hopes. No, he just couldn't let such a thing stand.

Turning to look at the small, isolated, and abandoned house where he had found shelter the previous night, Jessie walked back onto the porch and entered through the front door, where he found T. R. emotionally distraught, sobbing like a child.

Looking at T. R., Jessie said, "Are you thirsty?"

Nodding in the affirmative while trying to regain his composure, T. R. asked, "What can I do?"

"What do you mean?" Jessie replied as he retrieved his canteen from his saddle, which he had brought inside the previous night.

"You're right. You're right about everything," he said, looking Jessie directly in the eye.

Reaching out to him with the canteen, Jessie helped T. R. take a sip of water from the container, as his hands were still tied securely behind his back.

Swallowing the water, T. R. cleared his throat and said, "What can I do to make things right? There is nowhere to turn to for help. It's not like I can call and have the FBI arrive on the scene to deal with Peronne. It's like the Wild West out here now.

What no one sees, no one knows. As if there is anyone out there who would care, anyway. They've all got their own problems."

Dragging a small, wooden desk across the room, Jessie placed it directly in front of T. R., put a pencil and scrap of paper in front of him, and then walked around behind him and began untying his hands. Pausing before releasing the knot, Jessie said, "You're going to write down everything you know. You're going to write down every asset they have at their disposal. You're going to write down how many men they have. You're going to write down their schedules and routines. Everything you can think of. And if you try to make a move that makes me question your intentions, you'll die in that chair. Do you understand?"

"Yes, of course," T. R. replied.

His hands now free, T. R. rubbed his wrists, looked at Jessie, and took the pencil in hand. Walking around in front of T. R. in plain view, Jessie eased his Colt revolver out of his holster, flipped open the loading gate, half-cocked the hammer, and began to slowly and methodically rotate the cylinder, inspecting each cartridge as it turned.

Closing the loading gate and holstering his weapon, Jessie said, "Well, get started."

Nodding in reply, T. R. began to write. Watching for a few moments as T. R. worked his way down the piece of paper, Jessie nudged the curtain slightly to the side and looked out in front of the house, just in time to see a dark figure rush by the window. As he reached for his Colt, the window shattered as bullets began to fly into the room. Diving toward T. R., Jessie shoved his chair backward, knocking him to the floor and removing him from the direct line of fire as wood fragments filled the air from the impact of bullets on the wall behind them.

As the gunfire from outside the home ceased, a voice shouted, "Did you think you were just going to walk away from it all, Robertson? From everything we've done for you? From everything you've done? From everything you know? I always knew you wouldn't last, but I always thought you'd be weak and get yourself killed. I didn't think we were gonna have to do it for you. But here we are. You know how it works. Come on out and we'll let your friend with the horse live. If you make us come in and get you, we'll kill you both."

"They're gonna kill us both, no matter what," T. R. whispered to Jessie.

Lying on the floor next to him in a position of cover from the windows, Jessie reached over with his knife and cut T. R's feet lose, and said, "If you double-cross me, I promise I'll kill you, and I'll take my time doing it."

Nodding that he understood, T. R. pulled his legs off the chair and lay flat on the floor, saying, "Now what?"

"Keep them occupied for a moment," Jessie whispered in reply as he began to look around the room for an idea.

Shouting toward the now broken window, T. R. said, "It's not what it looks like, man. It's the guy we've been looking for. The one that killed the crazy old-timer. I caught him. I had to hole up here for the night, but I was going to bring him back to the chief today."

Looking back at Jessie, seeing his concerned and angry look, T. R. motioned to him in reassurance that he could trust him.

"Bull!" the man outside shouted. "Your tracks met up just over the hill from town. You came this way together."

"No, I followed him here from where I saw him on the ridge. I caught up with him just before he got to the house. You've got it all wrong, man."

As the men outside paused to discuss what T. R. had said, Jessie found a door hidden among the planks in the old, wood floor. Prying it up with his knife, he saw that it gave access to a crawlspace below the house that had apparently been used to store canned food by the previous occupants of the home. Motioning for T. R. to continue trying to reason with them, Jessie slipped beneath the home, closing the door above him as he disappeared below.

Seeing light shine through a screened ventilation opening on each of the foundation walls beneath the home, illuminating the dust particles dancing around in the stale air beneath the house, Jessie crawled over to the block foundation wall that faced the man giving the orders outside. Unable to get a complete view of the threat due to the limited line of sight offered by the opening, Jessie scanned the area as best he could, assuming their attackers were positioned behind the shed next to the house.

Hearing the shuffling of boots on the opposite side of the house, Jessie crawled through the dirt and dust beneath the home, occasionally feeling the crunch of an insect hidden in the darkness beneath his elbows. Looking out the screened vent on the back wall, he found a man dressed in the same tactical gear as T. R. standing just above the opening, his lower legs and dusty black books being the only thing visible from Jessie's vantage point.

In a static-filled and nearly unintelligible hand-held radio transmission, Jessie heard the words, "Take them out."

The man quietly replied that he understood by keying the mic twice.

Knowing that T. R. was in the room above, unarmed and alone, Jessie angled his rifle up toward the man with his stock held firmly against the ground, slowly pulling the trigger as the powerful .308 round discharged, nearly deafening Jessie as the shot was fired in the small, enclosed crawlspace. Disoriented from the intense ringing in his ears, Jessie saw the man writhing on the ground in pain with his hands on his groin as blood gushed from his body, his movements soon coming to a stop as his he bled out from his severe wound.

Gunfire now erupting from the opposite side of the house, tearing wildly into the wooden wall above the foundation, Jessie scurried back to the far wall, trying his best to get a view of the shooter. Seeing a muzzle flash coming from just around the corner of the shed, just out of sight, Jessie estimated the position of the shooter and began emptying the remaining contents of his twenty-round magazine into the flimsy structure. His bombardment of the thin walls of the shed with his powerful .308 rounds repeatedly penetrated the building, bringing the attack to an end. Scanning the area intently as the dust settled, he could see the barrel of an AR-15-style rifle on the ground, barely visible from around the corner of the structure where the shooter lay dead.

*Cover and concealment are two different things there, officer*, Jessie thought. Pausing for a moment, he attempted to listen for more movement as he quickly realized his attempts were futile as the shots fired from the enclosed space had left his eardrums throbbing with sharp, intense pain. Crawling back over to the crawlspace access door, Jessie forcefully pushed the door open and scanned the room with his rifle. Seeing only T. R., lying with his back to the far wall, behind the desk that he had positioned in front of him for cover, Jessie lowered his rifle and relaxed.

"You okay?" Jessie asked as he worked his jaw, attempting to alleviate some of the pain in his ears.

"Yeah... yeah, I'm all right," T. R. replied.

"Do you think there were more than two?"

"No. No, that's probably it. Unless it's a pretty big operation, the chief doesn't like to spread his resources too thin back in town. If they were just coming after me, two is all I would have imagined he would send. We've got to get out of here, though. They run a pretty tight ship and will notice when these two don't return when expected. That'll send up a red flag for sure. Chief

Peronne will send more next time. If he feels like there is a chink in his armor, he'll deal with it swiftly."

"Yep, I imagine so," Jessie said as he looked out the window in the direction of town. "Let's get what we can from your friends and get the hell out of here."

## Chapter Fourteen

Having stripped their attackers of their AR-15 patrol rifles, several loaded magazines of 5.56 NATO, two Smith & Wesson M&P .40 pistols, and two duty-belt-carried radios, Jessie looked at T. R., and said, “If you want to get to your family up north, you’d better get going. Take with you what you want for the journey. I can’t carry all of this, anyway. I just want to get it out of their hands and stash the extra somewhere in the event I need to come back for it.”

Looking down at the ground, pausing for a moment, T. R. responded, “I’ll go, but not yet. If I continue running away from the things I’ve done, the things I’ve been associated with, it will always haunt me. It will always be there. Even if I am lucky enough to simply blend back into my family as if it never happened... I... I just wouldn’t be able to live with myself. No, I need to do what I can to make things right before I go. I need to get rid of my old life before I try to start a new one. I’m staying with you.”

“I didn’t ask you to stay on with me,” Jessie replied sharply. “Quite frankly, I’m not sure I want or need your help. You want to make things right? I respect that, but if you couldn’t get past me, you probably can’t get past them. You’d be a liability to me.”

“No. No, that’s not true,” T. R. protested. “I can help. I know a few people in town who can help. There are a few good men that, if given the chance, I am certain would stand up to Peronne and his men.”

“But you are one of Peronne’s men. How would you know, what those you have helped to oppress, are willing and able to do?”

“Before I started working for the police—before I knew Peronne’s real goals—I had a few close friends in town. Jack

McGuigan was one. He and I were shooting buddies before... uh, before I joined the police department. After that, he just faded away as if he had no interest in me anymore. Then, once I realized what I had gotten into, I understood. But anyway, he is a real stand-up guy. Chief Peronne banned the private ownership of guns..."

"Like every good dictator," Jessie interrupted.

"Yeah, exactly. For the safety of the citizens, of course. As I was saying, Jack turned in a few rifles and pistols, but I knew he had more. I knew he must have squirreled a few things away, somewhere we couldn't find them when we searched his home."

"Wait, hold on..." Jessie said, holding his hand in the air to stop T. R. from continuing. "You mean to tell me that you were one of the officers who searched your former friend's home to confiscate his weapons?"

In a deflated tone, T. R. nodded and said, "Yes. Yes, I was."

"Peronne isn't the only treasonous scumbag in town," Jessie said with disgust in his voice. "And before you say it, I know, I know. You were just following orders," he said as he shook his head. "And now, you think a goose-stepping NAZI who 'was just following orders,' such as yourself who betrayed his friend, can just walk in there and convince him you're one of the good guys now? Hell, if he has half a brain, he'll think you're just setting him up on behalf of your former boss. I'd never trust you again. Hell, I'm not sure I can trust you now. I'll let you in on something," Jessie said as he squared off on T. R. with a hate-filled look in his eyes. "In my previous life, I was a sheriff before it all went down. I took that job very seriously. I took my oath very seriously. I would have gladly given my life for anyone in my county. You have no idea how badly I want to just kill you right now and move on with this on my own. What you've done, what a snake like Peronne has conned you into doing, is nothing less than a complete betrayal of your oath, and a complete betrayal of your fellow man. In America, at least as it was intended to be, the power is derived from the people. The people gave the government the right to enforce the laws that the people, through their representatives, put on the books. To take the role of a servant of the people and turn it into the role of a tyrant over the people, disgusts me beyond belief."

Shaking his head and waving his hands in protest, T. R. replied, "Trust me, I see your point clearly. I agree with every word you've said, but I can't turn back time. I can't undo what I've done or remake the decisions that led me to where I am right now. But if you want to do something about this, you can't do it alone. This is all we've got. We can't take down Peronne without help from inside the town. He's got an army, and most of them are all-in. They thrive in this new world, being the predators instead of the protectors."

"Is there anyone else within the department you can trust?" Jessie asked.

"Not really. It seemed that every time someone developed a conscious, they were the next one to have an *accident*."

Looking off into the distance, Jessie paused for a moment and said, "Don't give me a reason to regret this. You'll end up like your buddies over there," he said, motioning with his head in the direction of the dead officers. "The only thing that keeps me going in this world is a glimmer of hope, a faint little glimmer of hope that my future may bring. A hope that I know, deep down inside, is likely never going to come to fruition. But I keep going. I keep pressing on each day in search of that one thing. I've lost everything in this God-forsaken world. Don't you, for one second, make the mistake of thinking that I will allow myself to be double-crossed."

Feeling the tension in the air, T. R. replied, "Understood. So what is your hope? What are you searching for?"

"You'll have to earn my respect before I share something personal with you, and that's probably not going to happen. For now, it's all business. You work for me. You do what I say when I say it, and how I say it. I'm not your partner. I'm not your friend. You've got to earn those positions as well."

"So, you don't think people can change?" T. R. asked in a frustrated voice.

"Yes and no," Jessie replied. "A lot of people talk about being a changed man. It takes a lot more than words and good intentions for that to happen, though. You've got to be able to dig deep and stand up to whatever it is that led you astray. You can't just wish it away. You can't just say 'I don't do that anymore.' You've got to set things straight, in reality, not just words. Can people be forgiven, though? Of course. God knows who you really are on the inside, not just who you were in the past or the character you portray on the outside. It's the rest of us that need proof."

After a moment of awkward silence, Jessie said, "That's enough babbling on about redemption. Let's get a move on. We need to get somewhere safe where we can regroup, plan and observe. Got any ideas?"

Thinking to himself for a moment, T. R. replied with a grin, "Actually, yes. I do."

"And?" Jessie queried.

"Back home, when I was in my early twenties, some buddies and I would float down the river on a sunny Saturday afternoon on old dump truck inner tubes. We'd lash a cooler onto an extra tube and just drink beer and drift all day, waving at folks who lived on the riverbank as we floated past their backyards. We would use two pickup trucks. One to haul us upstream several miles, where we would begin our day of drinking beer and aimlessly floating, with another empty truck waiting for us at a selected location downstream. We would simply float from one truck to another and then drive back to get the first truck. If we were sober enough, that is."

"Go on..." Jessie said, interested on where the story was going.

"Anyway, Peronne has the roads and all of the main entryways into the city pretty well controlled. However, the Pecos River, especially at night, may be a good way in. They watch it from a distance when doing patrols, but no one actually walks the bank. If we can work our way around to the northwest and intercept the Pecos River, and if we can find something that will work as a float, we can drift into town under the cover of darkness. The Pecos River heads directly into town from the west until it reaches a point where it makes a turn to the south. On the north bank of the river at the bend, there's a narrow strip of land between the canal and the river that is mostly brush and trees, with only one house I can think of. We can beach our tubes and hide them in the brush. With their eyes on the roads and traditional access points, we may be able to slip into town and work our way to Jack's place."

"How far into town is Jack, and how far from the nearest concentration of police assets is he?" Jessie asked, intrigued by the idea.

"City Hall is a good distance away, but he's basically just a block from the post office. They use that building as a storage facility due to the fact that it was built to be naturally secure. They keep the assets taken from all of the ambush sites there."

"Sounds like that's Peronne's bank." Jessie snarled.

"Yeah, basically," T. R. replied. "On the bright side, any of the officers at the post office will be there for the primary duty of defending the facility. It's not a launching point of patrols or operations. It can be a good indicator of their current protective posture, though. Also, I can estimate how many officers are potentially on patrol based on how many are guarding the facility."

"Is that where he keeps the women and children he takes from the ambushes? Or is that elsewhere?"

"Typically, the people who are taken aren't kept in Fort Sumner very long. Peronne has to keep up an image within the town, or at least he thinks he does. He tries to keep such things under wraps. He's living this delusion that if he keeps up the appearance of being the legitimate government of Fort Sumner and with the people's best interests at heart, that people will eventually start to see things that way. Like I said, though, he's delusional. Everyone in town knows what he's done and what he's up to. They'll never forget. Some are okay with it because they get something out of it, but most are just biding their time."

"Biding their time for what?"

"Nothing specific," T. R. replied as he swatted at a mosquito. "Damn bugs are gonna be thick this year," he said. "Anyway, they just figure it won't go on forever. But in regards to the people taken during the ambushes, they are flown out or transported by road within a day of their capture. Peronne typically doesn't take in anyone he doesn't put a trade value on, and they definitely don't get brought to town if they don't have value."

"Did you participate in any of the ambushes?" Jessie asked. "And don't lie to me."

"No. Not at all," T. R. quickly replied. "Peronne has a special team for that. They're his inner circle, and they're cut from the same cloth as him. No, those guys didn't care for me much. I was mostly utilized for patrols and watch standing within the town."

Piecing together everything T. R. was saying in his mind, Jessie said, "On the east side of town, I came across several vehicles that looked as if they had been taken down by an ambush. The previous night, I heard an exchange of gunfire from my camp. That's what led me there the next morning. One of the vehicles was a minivan that appeared to have been transporting several small children. There were several dead adult civilians at the scene and one dead officer..."

"Picoulas," T. R. interrupted.

"What?"

"The officer that was killed was Picoulas. Dave Picoulas. He was kind of an ass, so it didn't hurt my feelings any when I heard," T. R. replied.

"So you know about that hit, then?" asked Jessie.

"I know it happened, but not any specifics. One thing I can tell you, though, is that Peronne's Go-team made a run to the airport the next morning. With who or what, I don't know. I did overhear some of the guys joking about a woman, though."

"What about a woman?" Jessie asked.

"Barnes... he's one of Peronne's lap dogs, was joking about some woman they had gotten the opportunity to have a little fun with while she was drugged out of her mind. That was the straw that broke the camel's back for me. That's why I finally left. What those bastards did while they were outside of town was one thing, but the fact that they were now bringing it back to town with them... well, that was my cue to leave. What if they were having their way with some woman and I was around? Could I just look the other way? I just couldn't deal with the thought of that."

"I thought you said they didn't keep people in town?"

"They usually don't. That was a first that I know of. I don't know what Peronne has or had in mind, but I didn't want to be around for it."

"Is she still there? Is she okay?" Jessie asked.

"I'm not sure. Like I said, that was the first I had even heard about it, and I punched out that night. If we can get into town, though, and if we can get to Jack, he may have a clue. His daughter, Angela, works for City Hall. She's a clerk of some sort now. She was a driver's licensing examiner for the state before it all started, so I guess it was an easy transition for her to work in public service. Anyway, I'm sure she keeps him up to speed on the goings on, at least to the extent she is aware."

Confused by what seemed to him to be contradictions, Jessie asked, "If this Jack guy is so against Peronne and what he does, why does he allow his daughter to work for him?"

"She doesn't actually work for Peronne directly, just for the city. Granted, it's a small city, so she does have to interact with him on occasion, but I'd imagine Jack would rather have her in a safe place and in the know. Knowledge is not only power; it can mean security as well. Plus, Peronne generally doesn't hurt his own people. He needs loyalty to stay in control. Once I began to work for the department, and Jack started giving me the cold shoulder, I never personally spoke with her other than just being cordial in passing."

Looking at his watch and comparing it to the position of the sun, Jessie exhaled deeply and said reluctantly, "Okay, we'll go in together. Let's get a move on before we find ourselves on the run again. Let's get old Eli saddled up and get the extra gear loaded up. You and I can walk, and he can haul the gear. Although I would love to take my time to observe and plan, I have a feeling our window of opportunity is getting narrower with each passing moment. As soon as they realize what happened to your former cohorts they sent after you, the game will start to change."

## Chapter Fifteen

Walking over to the record player while Leina sat quietly in the leather chair by the bookshelf, Chief Peronne lifted the needle off the record spinning on the turntable and removed it, carefully putting it away. Blowing the dust off another record that he carefully removed from an old, well-worn album cover, he placed it gently on the turntable and began to watch it spin as he lowered the needle. “You’re gonna love this one,” he said, appearing to be lost in the music.

Closing his eyes as he listened intently to the crackle through the speakers of the old machine, he smiled as the saxophone and old upright bass began to belt out his favorite tune, followed by the smooth and hypnotic sound of an electric guitar that was clearly in very skilled hands. “It’s food for the soul,” he said as he swayed with the rhythm and the beat.

Looking the bookshelf over as she took another sip of wine, Leina noticed it was full of the great classics of modern literature, as well as Greek philosophy and books on the art of war.

As her eyes scanned each volume, her thoughts were interrupted by the sounds of his footsteps coming closer and his voice, saying, “Feel free to take any of them to read.”

“You’ve got quite a collection,” she said smartly.

With a smug look on his face, he opened his mouth to reply just as she asked, “Did you acquire them all yourself, or did they belong to someone else before the collapse?”

Pausing for a moment, his smile fading from view, Chief Peronne said, “That’s why we need you around here.”

“Why?” she asked.

“Because you’re a survivor. That’s why you’ve kept yourself and your children alive for so long. You can’t let even one moment go by without asserting some level of control. You feel the need to guide even the simplest conversation. I admire that. Strength is what this world needs most of all. Weakness is what got us into the mess."

"Weakness, betrayal, and treachery," she replied, taking a sip of wine.

"Indeed," he replied calmly, increasing the sharpness of his gaze. "Back to my point, though. We need someone like you around here. I can offer you a home to live in, and although we don't have a traditional monetary system for trade, I can offer you food, clothing, and everything you'll need."

"And for the children?"

"Of course, the children," he replied. "The children can go to school with the other kids and live about as normal a life as one could expect these days."

"Don't you mean *we*?" she asked, looking him directly in the eye.

Confused by her statement, he said, "Excuse me? I don't follow."

"Don't you mean *we,* as in the residents of the town? You keep saying *I*. I thought as a police officer, even the chief of police, that you were simply one of the town's civil servants. Does what you are offering me belong to you, or the townspeople?"

Placing his glass on the table, he turned to her and said in a calm and collected voice, "Look, I respect your tenacity, but you don't need to pick apart every word I say. Arguing over semantics isn't going to get us anywhere. I'm trying to do something good for you."

"All I want from you is to stop playing games and bring back my children."

Taking a seat across from her, placing his elbows on his knees and leaning forward, he began to speak, as Leina was distracted by a dizzy feeling that started to come over her. *Was it the wine?* she thought, looking at her glass. *It has been a while since I've had a drink.*

Tuning back into his words, she could tell that Chief Peronne was seemingly becoming more agitated as he spoke, saying, "Look, I brought you here to this beautiful house. I offered you expensive wine—which is a real luxury these days that not many people can acquire. I've played beautiful music for you from antique and hard-to-find albums. And I've offered you a life and a future that many women around the world would literally kill for today. And how do you show your thanks? You repay me with disrespect..."

Her vision now becoming blurry, she tuned out his words for a moment as she tried to get a grip on herself. Interrupting his childish rant, she demanded, "Where are the children? Stop... stop playing games and bring them to me," she said as the room began to spin.

Standing in front of her, Chief Peronne walked over to her and said, "That's enough of that. You're not in a position to keep making demands. And quite frankly, I'm tired of hearing them."

A feeling of warmth and numbness began to come over her as she looked at her glass. "You bastard!" she shouted, splashing him in the face with its remaining contents.

Picking up a decorative towel from an elegant silver serving tray next to the bottle of wine, he wiped his face, and with a crooked smile said, "It's clear I may not get what I want from you, but I'll sure as hell take what I need."

## Chapter Sixteen

As the chill of the cool night's breeze blew across Jessie's face, he paused in a crouching position, looking and listening for any activity up ahead. Having worked their way around Fort Sumner at a safe distance, arcing around to the north and northwest, Jessie and T. R. were finally in a position to make their move into the town.

Looking back toward T. R.'s last known position, Jessie signaled for him to hold there. Working his way back to T. R. through the brush of the surrounding area, Jessie arrived to find T. R. waiting patiently with Eli as he had been instructed.

"Are you ready to do this?" Jessie asked as if to offer T. R. one final opportunity to change his mind.

"Yes, sir," T. R. replied sharply.

"You know we're not going to just walk out of there, right? At some point, it's gonna get rough. Someone is gonna get killed. Who that someone is, remains to be seen. Are you sure you're up to walking right into the middle of it all, knowing the advantages they have?"

"Without question," T. R. replied.

"Well, let me take care of something first," Jessie said as he walked over to Eli and began to scratch him on the top of his head and underneath his chin. "Eli, old boy," Jessie said with fondness and affection in his voice. "I don't know where things are gonna go from here. If I see you again, you can be rest assured you'll always have a home with me. But just in case I don't return, I want you to have a fighting chance," he said as he removed Eli's harness.

Walking around to the saddle, Jessie removed the load that Eli had dutifully carried and then gently slipped the saddle off of him as well. "Go on, boy. I'm sure you can find plenty to eat out there," he said, walking back in front of him and scratching him under the chin for what could be the last time. "Just do me a favor. Stay away from people, if you can. We're the most dangerous predator out there. Unlike a wolf or a mountain lion, whose motivations are always consistent and clear, a man's motives can never be trusted, unless, of course, that trust is earned. Now, go. Go live out your retirement in freedom." he said, giving Eli a swat on the rear end, running him off into the darkness and away from the dangers of town.

"You don't think we're gonna need him when it's over?" T. R. asked.

"That wouldn't be fair to him. We've got about as much of a chance of making it back to him in one piece as he does of picking up a rifle and joining us. No, if something were to happen to us, I want Eli to live out his final days as he sees fit. Leaving him out here, tied to a tree to starve to death while he waits for us to return would be cruel. There's just too many ways this can all go wrong to leave him in that kind of a situation."

Nodding in agreement, T. R. asked, "So, what now? What's the plan?"

"It's your plan from here. You know the river. You know our adversary. I'm second guessing the floating idea, though."

"What do you mean?" T. R. asked, confused as to what Jessie meant.

"I'd feel like a sitting duck, floating along at the mercy of the current, just waiting to be shot. How deep is the river on average?"

"I think it averages eight feet deep below the Lake Sumner dam, but it's quite shallow in many places."

"Eight feet in the center, right? How's the gradient of the riverbank? Is it steep or shallow?"

"Mostly shallow," T. R. replied. "I believe you could walk out into most of it until it got too deep, but that's not an educated answer. That's a casual observer's answer."

"Let's use the river as our access point, as you recommended, but let's go in on foot, wading in the shallows, with the ability to disappear quickly under the cover of the water if need be. It will be slower going, but I have a feeling it would be much safer and stealthier than floating down the middle of the river, potentially drifting right in front of trouble with little recourse."

Thinking it over for a moment, T. R. nodded in agreement and said, "That sounds like a plan."

"Great," Jessie replied. "You take point from here. The river, according to my estimations based on our approximate position in relation to this map, is about a half mile up ahead. We should intercept it a mile or so north of the edge of town. We'll hike down the riverbank until we get close, and then we can slip into the water with our rifles across our shoulders or on our heads, and just allow ourselves to drift with the current, guided by our feet and the river bottom. Again, since you know the environment and the threat, you take point. We'll exit the water at a location that you feel is advantageous."

"Roger that," T. R. replied as he slung his AR15 over his shoulder, beginning his advancement toward the river.

"Oh, and by the way," Jessie said, getting T. R.'s attention.

Turning back to see what Jessie had to say, T. R. replied, "What's up?"

"Don't forget to switch your safety off this time. If it's a big enough threat to justify pointing your rifle at it, it's a big enough threat to be prepared and configured to shoot."

With a half-hearted chuckle, T. R. replied, "Yeah, right," as he turned and headed off into the darkness toward the river to the southwest of their position.

~~~~

Approaching the river, barely visible from the near lack of moonlight due to a high cloud layer moving into the area, T. R. motioned for Jessie to advance toward his position and to rally on him. Unsure if Jessie had seen his signal in the darkness of the night, he focused intently, trying to catch a glimpse of movement in the direction from which he came.

"What's up?" Jessie whispered, approaching T. R. from the side.

Startled, T. R. whispered, "Holy crap, man! I thought you were behind me."

"I was behind you," Jessie replied. "Behind you is that way," he said, pointing off in the darkness.

"It's so damn dark I guess I lost my bearings. Anyway, the river is just up ahead. You can hear the water flowing if you listen."

"Yeah, I hear it," Jessie replied. Removing his Colt from its holster, Jessie tied a piece of paracord around the trigger guard and then tied the pistol around his neck, tucking it inside his shirt. Next, removing his rifle's sling from his shoulder, Jessie put his AR-10 across the back of his neck, holding the barrel with his left hand and the stock with his right. He wrapped the slack of the sling around his right fist, ensuring that he would maintain his grip on the weapon if troubles were to arise.

"You'd better get yourself together for fighting from the neck up," he said to T. R. "You'll want the things you need to be able to get to near the surface, not only to keep them safe, but to have them readily accessible, and so that they don't get lost. The last thing I would want to do is drop my pistol underwater while trying to draw it from the holster."
~~~~

"I think my pistol will be fine," T. R. replied. "But I'll keep my rifle high and dry."

"Are you ready?" Jessie asked.

"As ready as I'll ever be. Let's get on with it," T. R. said as he turned and slipped off into the brush in the direction of the river.

Arriving at the river's edge, T. R. turned to make sure Jessie was behind him. With a nod, he then slipped quietly into the water with Jessie approximately ten yards behind.

Working their way downstream toward town, the riverbank transitioned from a mix of sandy stone and mud to thick, dense brush and vegetation that extended over the river's edge and into the water, forcing both men further into the river, bringing the water level up to their chests. With the sense of touch alone to navigate river bottom below, T. R.'s right foot slipped into a hole, tripping him, forcing him to slide backward and underneath the water. As his body slid backward, feet-first downstream, the current swept him off his feet, taking him below. Disoriented by the darkness and the sudden fall, T. R. struggled to get solid footing in an attempt to slow his current-induced slide into the deeper center of the river.

Finally securing his footing, T. R. shoved off the river's bottom with both feet, only to find that he was entangled in something. With panic now setting in, he released his grip on his rifle and began to feel around in the total darkness, to find a rope of some sort that had become tangled between his clothing and his holster. Yanking on it fiercely, but to no avail, he reached for his knife in a panicked attempt to cut himself free. In his disoriented and frightened state, he fumbled the knife, allowing the current to wash it free from his grip.

At the surface, Jessie had heard T. R. slip and fall beneath the water but was unable to see him in the absence of light. "Hey," he whispered. "Are you okay?"

Hearing no response, Jessie tried his best to focus his eyes in the near total darkness. Hearing rustling off to his left in the brush along the side of the riverbank. Quickly bringing his rifle over his head, Jessie flipped the selector switch to the fire position and trained his barrel on the source of the noise.

Realizing that the noise was not a human threat, Jessie worked his way to it, following the sounds of the rustling branches until he felt a taut line that reached from beneath the water and was tied off to one of the thick branches of the brush. Feeling the force being applied to the line from underneath the water, Jessie quickly drew his knife and slashed at the rope, immediately cutting it, releasing the tension.

Beneath the water, as T. R.'s desperate attempts to free himself had all failed and he was unable to hold his breath any longer, he released the air held within his lungs and began to choke as he felt the tension in the line release and go slack. Moving again with the current, the line pulled against him, still snagged to his holster, causing the current to wash him to the far side of the river where the rope was still secured.

Pushing toward the surface with all of his might, his head emerged as he began immediately gasping for air and coughing violently. Crawling up onto the rocky and sandy shore on the far side of the river, T. R. vomited profusely, pumping water from his stomach and clearing his throat. "Damn it to hell," he mumbled while coughing hoarsely.

Hearing a whistle from the far side of the river, he muttered, "Okay... I'm... I'm okay."

Feeling around his holster, T. R. snagged something sharp with his hand, puncturing his skin. "Damn it," he said aloud as he winced in pain, quickly pulling back his hand. Feeling around slowly, he felt fishhooks and said, "It's a damn trotline. Crap. I was almost killed by a damn trotline. Get it together!" he said as if scolding himself.

From the far side of the riverbank, T. R. could hear Jessie faintly saying, "Report."

"I'm okay," he answered. "It's too deep here to swim across with all this gear. I'll stay on this side of the river for a while until it shallows out again, then I'll cross back over."

"Roger that," Jessie replied.

Once T. R. had successfully worked the fishhook lose from his holster, the two once again began working their way downstream toward town.

~~~~

Approximately a mile downstream from the site of T. R.'s close call, the river widened and provided suitable shallows with several gravel bars, allowing T. R. to cross.

Meeting back up with Jessie, T. R. said, "Around the next bend is the railroad bridge that spans the river. That's one of the points where there is likely a lookout, or at a minimum, a regular patrol. We need to get out of the water here and head off in that direction," he said as he pointed toward the east. "There are several dry washes between here and town that are full of brush and trees. They fill with water when the water level in the river is high. They should be dry now, but we can use them as cover as we work our way into town."

Patting T. R. on the shoulder, Jessie said, "Lead the way."
~~~~

## Chapter Seventeen

Following T. R., approximately twenty yards in trail, Jessie saw him give the hold signal as they approached the outskirts of town. With a few of the buildings having operational electric lights, Jessie listened for the sound of a generator, knowing that the city could not be on the previously existing regional electrical grid that had been severely damaged as a target of the attacks.

Seeing T. R. motion for him to continue, Jessie joined up with him to survey the area ahead.

"That's Sunnyside Avenue," T. R. whispered as he pointed.

Seeing a vehicle's headlights come around the corner of a building off in the distance, he signaled for Jessie to get down and whispered softly, "They should pass on by. Just hold tight until I say. I would assume this is a routine patrol. This is one of the standard routes. They come down Rice Avenue, and then make a turn to Sunnyside, then Dunn, and on to West Sumner Avenue. From there, they follow the perimeter of town. After they pass, we'll make our move toward Jack's home, which is just two blocks up from Sunnyside Avenue."

Nodding in reply, Jessie watched as the patrol approached their position. Thoughts raced through his mind about the man he had teamed up with for this dangerous and potentially deadly undertaking. Could he be trusted? As he reached down and placed his hand on his knife, he thought to himself, *All he would have to do is simply stand up and wave his buddies over to us. Then, he could come up with some bullsh— story about how he led me here, to get his butt out of the bind he's found himself in. If this son-of-a-b— so much as flinches when they get close, I'll take him out.*

Slowing and scanning the area with their spotlight, the men in the desert tan-painted SUV pulled to a stop only twenty yards from Jessie and T. R.'s position, placing the vehicle in park, but keeping the engine running.

As the passenger door opened and one of the men, dressed in the same tactical gear as T. R., stepped out of the vehicle, Jessie began to draw his knife from his sheath as T. R. looked back at Jessie, his eyes darting down to Jessie's hand.

Turning back to the threat in front of them, T. R. slowly lifted his rifle into a ready position, with his muzzle pointed at the man exiting the vehicle.

After a moment, the man turned and said something to his partner, which was unintelligible to Jessie and T. R., prompting the driver of the vehicle to exit as well. *Here we go,* Jessie thought as he removed his hand from his knife and raised his rifle in preparation for what he assumed would come next. *This sure didn't take long.*

Walking over to his partner, the driver of the vehicle reached into his pocket, removing a pack of cigarettes, handing one to the other man. Jessie watched as the two casually leaned back against the vehicle, seemingly enjoying their smoke break. *I wonder where those bastards got their smokes,* he thought. *From an unsuspecting traveler, no doubt.*

After several tense moments, watching and waiting, the men got back in their vehicle and drove away, scanning with their searchlight as they went. Moving on up to T. R., Jessie said, "You have no idea how bad I wanted to smoke those bastards."

"It looked to me like I was on your list as well," T. R. replied, glancing down at Jessie's knife.

"You would have been if I was given a good enough reason," Jessie replied. "So far so good, though. Enough chatting. Let's get moving. What's the plan?"

"Jack's place is just a few blocks up, like I said. That's about as far as my plan goes. I'm really not sure how to approach the situation. It's not like we can just walk up and knock on his door. There are too many eyes in this town. There are a lot of good people here, but there are a few that act as Peronne's eyes and ears in exchange for a little extra protection or favor."

"We'll figure something out," Jessie replied. "Let's just get there."

With a nod, T. R. signaled for Jessie to hold his position as he made his move across Sumner Avenue, continuing until he could take visual cover behind a section of fence on the far side of the road. Jessie watched as T. R. signaled him to join him on the other side. Looking around carefully, Jessie emerged from a small cluster of trees and began to quickly cross the street as he caught movement out of the corner of his eye, off to his left flank. Turning toward the potential threat, Jessie rocked his AR-10 forty-five degrees to the side, looking through his offset backup iron sites. Flipping the selector switch on his rifle from safe to semi-auto, his sights settled on the movement as his finger twitched and his heart raced.

"Ah, damn it. Stupid cat!" he whispered aloud to himself as he watched a housecat dart off into the shadows.

Reaching T. R.'s position, T. R. greeted him with a chuckle, saying quietly, "Was the cat on your list, too?"

"My list is subject to change at a second's notice," Jessie replied.

"So, anyway," T. R. continued, "Jack's house is on the corner of Richards and Sharp Street, right across from Saint Anthony's. Saint Anthony's is the building with its exterior lights on, up the street and on the right."

"Is that a church?" Jessie asked.

"Yeah," replied T. R. "Peronne provides them with electricity from the generators that power the critical facilities in town. It's one of his good deeds to appease the residents. That, and to not make it such a big deal that he supplies electricity from the city's emergency power to his own home—for security reasons, of course."

"Of course," Jessie replied, returning the sarcastic sentiment.

Pointing to the south-facing fence surrounding Jack's home, T. R. said, "With the light from the church on the north side, our best bet is to enter Jack's yard from the south-side, and then work our way to the house in the darkness."

Simply nodding in reply, T. R. and Jessie began edging their way from the fence alongside Sumner Avenue toward Jack McGuigan's home, using a tactical bound, providing cover for each other as they went. Arriving at the six-foot-tall, wooden privacy fence running along the south-facing edge of Jack's property, Jessie held his position, allowing T. R. to join up with him.

Tapping Jessie on the shoulder, T. R. whispered, "Keep an eye out while I look for a way in."

With a nod, Jessie turned his attentions to their surroundings, while T. R. began checking the integrity of each of the fence boards until finding one that appeared looser than the rest. Pulling the bottom of the board free, he pulled out and upward, pulling at the nails that held the board at the top loose, but leaving them holding the board in place. Pulling on the board to the left of his now small access hole, finding it held tightly in place, T. R. moved to the board to its right, working it loose after a few good tugs.

As Jessie scanned the area, he looked to his left to check on T. R.'s status, only to see that he was gone, "What the...? Hey?" he whispered.

Poking his head through the hole in the fence, T. R. said, "Come on in. Just pull the boards back into place behind you."

Following T. R.'s lead, Jessie squeezed his way through the small opening and into the backyard of the home. Pulling the board back into position, having never been removed from the upper nails holding it in place, he masked their entry point as best he could.

"I think you'd better lead the way from here," T. R. sheepishly said. "I don't think someone dressed like me, crawling around his home in the middle of the night, would go over very well."

"I'd venture to guess that any man crawling around someone's home in the middle of the night wouldn't go over very well," Jessie replied. "Besides, it's not like I can put him at ease by telling him that someone who turned on him and his people sent me. Just go knock on the back door and talk to him like a man. Own up to it. Look him in the eye and tell him the truth. It's the only way this is going to work."

Nodding in agreement, T. R. said, "Okay. Well, keep an eye out. The patrols go by the church every so often."

Slipping up to the home, T. R. raised his hand and began to knock on the door as he was startled by the sounds of a small dog barking feverishly on the other side of a window screen, just to the right of the back door.

Flinching from the unexpected bark, T. R. turned toward the sound, only to hear the door swing open, and to feel a blunt object strike him in the face, knocking him to the ground. Looking up, dazed and confused, he reached for his sidearm as he saw the butt of a pump shotgun being thrust down at his face by the very man he had come to see.

Just as the shotgun was about to make contact, Jessie tackled the man to the ground, saving T. R. from what would have been a violent blow to the face. "No!" Jessie said sternly through gritted teeth. "He's here to talk. We're here to talk... and get some help."

Just then, the little dog came barreling out of the back door, pouncing on T. R., biting down on his vest and shaking side to side. Knocking the dog off him, they heard a woman's voice yell, "Tyke! No! Don't hurt him!"

Climbing to his knees, T. R. pushed the little dog away once more, shouting, "Get it off! Angela, get him off!"

"T. R.?" she queried, surprised that it was him.

"Yeah, it's that treasonous son-of-a-b—!" her father Jack shouted.

"Sir, calm down. He's with me, and we're here for a good reason. Hear us out. We need to get inside and work this out before Peronne's men catch wind of what's going on."

"I don't give a damn!" Jack shouted. "I'll tell them you were breaking into our home in the middle of the night. You're probably the bastard they're looking for anyway."

"Do you want them to see that you still have a gun in this house?" Jessie asked. "Isn't that forbidden? What else will they find when they search your home because of it?"

"They'll find Tyke, Dad. He's right."

Relaxing his struggle, Jack looked at T. R. and said, "I don't want that son-of-a-b— in my home."

"It's him or the rest of Peronne's men. Your call," Jessie said, making Jack's choices clear.

Pausing for a moment to think things through, Jack reluctantly replied, "You'd better keep him out of my reach. I can't make any promises as to what I'll do if I get my hands on him."

"I understand completely," Jessie said as he got off the man and reached out with his hand to help him up.

Refusing the assistance with a defiant attitude, Jack stood up, dusted himself off, and said, "Get in the house, but keep your hands where I can see them."

"Yes, sir," replied Jessie.

Picking up the dog, Angela said, “Hurry up, before they come,” as she hurried into the home.

## Chapter Eighteen

Once inside the home, Jack shouted through the house, "Angela, get in here."

Running into the room, carrying a lantern-style candle holder to light her way, she said, "I'm right here. I was just putting Tyke in the basement.

Handing her the shotgun, Jack said, "Keep an eye on them for a minute while I check the front."

Taking the shotgun, Angela watched as her father went through the home, looking out of each of the windows as he went. Ducking around the corner for a moment, he reappeared with a 9mm Springfield XD pistol with a frame-mounted combination laser/flashlight.

"I don't see any of their friends out there," Jack said to Angela. "You got Tyke taken care of?"

"Yes, he's in the basement," she replied.

Looking at both T. R. and Jessie with an icy-cold stare, he then said, "If you bring Peronne down on us, and she loses that dog, I'll kill you both."

Confused, Jessie said, "Loses the dog? What do you mean?"

"Do you not know anything?" Jack said with contempt in his voice. Motioning toward T. R. with his pistol, he added, "Ask your buddy here."

Clearing his throat, T. R. sheepishly said, "Peronne has declared control over the food resources in town."

"Like any good dictator," Jessie interjected.

"Yeah, exactly," T. R. replied. "Well, anyway, since he lays claim to control of redistribution of our food supplies, as well as just about everything else, he banned the ownership of non-agricultural animals. People can have chickens, sheep, cattle, goats, etc., but no dogs or cats. He says they don't earn their keep, and we can't afford the extra mouths to feed."

"Right," said Jack as he moved the kitchen curtain out of the way with the barrel of his pistol, again looking outside to scan the area. Lighting several extra candles to better illuminate the room, he added, "So like I said, if you bring Peronne down on us, and they take her dog, Tyke, they'll kill him, and for that, I'll kill you. That dog is a member of this family and I will treat his loss as such. Do you understand me?" he said with a clenched jaw, waving the pistol back and forth between the two men. "I know who this traitor is, but who are you?" Jack asked Jessie.

"My name is Jessie Townsend. Before it all went down, I was the sheriff of Montezuma County in Colorado. To save you the details, after the collapse, I lost everything—my wife, children, everything. I was on my way east to find my sister. She's all I have left in this world. Or, at least, I hope I still have her."

Pausing momentarily, thinking of his sister, Jessie snapped back into the moment, saying, "Anyway, as I was passing through the area, I worked my way around to the north in order to avoid the town and any threats it may contain. When I got to the Red Lake area, I came across what appeared to have been an ambush. It was recent, as in the evening before, with the bodies of the victims still strewn about. One of the vehicles contained signs that the victims had been traveling with small children."

Clearing his throat, Jessie continued, "I just couldn't live with myself if I just let it go and kept going, so I gave the dead their proper respects and began to watch the town from a distance. That's where I bumped into him" he said, gesturing toward T. R. "He says he's had enough of Peronne and was running away to link up with his family in Oklahoma. He seems legit, but I've been keeping my eye on him, hoping I can trust him," Jessie said, getting his point across to both T. R. and Jack.

Looking Jack squarely in the eye, Jessie added, "He said your daughter works at City Hall and may have some information to help us figure out what happened to anyone who might have been taken during the ambush."

As Angela started to answer, Jack interrupted, saying, "So, let me get this straight. A total stranger, who was just passing by, is risking his neck to check on other total strangers that might not even be alive? Why the hell would you do that?"

"Only worrying about ourselves is what got us into this mess," Jessie replied. "You've got no right to complain about the world around you if you're not gonna be man enough to do something about it. Thinking of my own children, and how if they were still alive and something happened to me, I would want someone to try to lend them a hand. Besides, like I said, I lost everything. What do I have to lose?"

"Your life," Jack replied.

"There's not much value in that if it's not a life well lived," Jessie quickly responded. "Staying on the run isn't a life, it's an existence."

"So, you're the one?" Angela said, looking at T. R., continuing what she was going to say before she was interrupted.

"The one?" Jack enquired.

"I overheard some of the men saying that one of the officers deserted. They were saying they were really gonna mess him up when they found him."

"They've tried that already," said Jessie. "It didn't work out for them."

"Sounds like you're really stirring up a mess," replied Jack.

"You've already got a mess," Jessie stated. "The only thing is, no one is doing anything about it."

Seeming to take offense at Jessie's statement, Jack started to reply as T. R. interjected, "Look, the reason we are here is that I thought Angela might have seen or heard something."

"Seen or heard what?" she asked.

"Barnes was joking about some woman they were keeping somewhere, who, at least from the sound of it, wasn't being treated very lady-like, to say the least. The timing of which coincides with the timing of what Jessie says happened east of town."

Thinking for a moment, she added, "I've not heard anything directly, but now that you mention it, Rosa had been taking things back and forth to the detention center from Peronne's home. That sort of lines up with what you are saying."

"Things? What sort of things?" T. R. asked.

"Laundry, food, bedding, and such," she replied. "I didn't really think much of it at the time. I just assumed it was for officers on overnight duty somewhere. It might be nothing, but it also might be what you are talking about."

"Why would they be keeping someone against their will like that?" Jack asked. "Well, I guess I can think of a few reasons they would be keeping a woman, based on human nature alone, but why the children?"

Taking a deep breath, T. R. spoke up and said, "Let me explain to you exactly what I know, and where some of the supplies Peronne keeps pumping into the town come from."

For the next few minutes, T. R. explained to Jack and Angela what he had previously told Jessie about how Chief Peronne lures unsuspecting travelers to the outskirts of Fort Sumner in order to steal their supplies, and often times their freedom, trading them to a human-trafficking ring with which Peronne has allegiance.

Before anyone else could respond, Jack interrupted, saying, "I've got to talk to my daughter in private for a moment. You two wait right here. Don't go anywhere and don't touch anything. Understood?"

"Yes, sir," Jessie replied. "Your home, your castle."

As Jack and Angela left the room, T. R. looked at Jessie and said, "Well, that went better than I expected."

With a chuckle, Jessie said, "It ain't over yet. He might just be going to get his *guttin'* knife. You might end up being dog food for Tyke."

"Ha, ha," T. R. responded sarcastically.

A few moments later, Jack and Angela came back into the room carrying several towels and neatly folded sets of men's clothing. "Here," Jack said, tossing them each a set of clothes. "You both look like you're roughly my size. Get out of those wet clothes. You're getting my kitchen floor all wet. You'll sleep in the basement tonight. Tomorrow, Angela will see what she can find out, and we'll go from there about how we're gonna deal with this. If she verifies what you say, well, we want to help. We've had about enough of the goings on around here. But if what you say isn't true, well, you've opened a can of worms for yourselves. You've picked the wrong guy to con if you're pullin' a con."

"That sounds good to us," Jessie replied. "Just keep in mind that time is of the essence in a situation like this. If they are keeping someone, especially children, the longer this drags on, the less likely there will be a good outcome and the less likely it will be that we or anyone else will find them."

"Yeah, well, I don't think I can take things around here much longer anyway. We've been silently biding our time, until a reason to make a move presented itself. If what you say is true, we have our reason. Now, you two get changed and then follow me. Angela, I've got this, you go on back to bed."

Giving her father a hug, Angela did as he asked, leaving Jack, T. R. and Jessie alone in the kitchen. As Jessie and T. R.

began to change clothes, Jack saw Jessie's Colt Single Action Army hanging from the paracord rope around Jessie's neck.

"Are you tryin' to be sneaky or something? Hiding that thing like that?" he asked.

"No, sir," Jessie replied. "I just didn't want to lose my only remaining family heirloom in the river."

"Can't say I blame you there," Jack replied.

Once the men had changed into dry clothes, Jack returned to the kitchen, and said, "Okay. Now, I can't believe I'm gonna let you go down to where I'm about to take you, but we need to be able to keep this little slumber party discreet. I guess what I'm trying to say is, I won't be double-crossed. You, sir," he said looking at Jessie, "I don't know you from Adam, and T. R., well, I've got plenty reasons not to put a damn bit of faith in what you say. It hurt me bad when you teamed up with the bastard that's keeping the rest of us down. I don't care if it seemed like your only option at the time. I'll never forget the side you chose to take. So both of you, forgive me if I'm less than the perfect host. And keep in mind, my continued willingness to be a host is based on whether or not what you say pans out to be the truth. If not, well, we'll go from there."

Turning to walk down the hall, he said, "Now, follow me and try to be quiet. Angela has to get up in the morning to go to work, and if you wake Tyke, he'll keep her up all night."

"What kind of dog is Tyke?" Jessie asked. "All I've had in the past are livestock guardian dogs, so I'm not familiar with the smaller breeds."

"He's a miniature schnauzer, and like I said, he's basically family to her. I'll treat things that way if anything happens to him."

Following Jack down a narrow set of stairs that were behind what seemed like a closet door, Jessie noticed old family portraits of a woman and a young boy along with Jack and

Angela spanning what appeared to be the entirety of what would have been Angela's childhood, hanging on the wall, descending with the stairs. He could only assume that it was Jack's wife and a brother of Angela's, but didn't want to ask, given the tension in their presence. Knowing all too well the pain of such a loss, if that were to be the case, Jessie understood Jack's lack of trust and fierce attitude in regards to protecting his family. Thinking back to the Walkers' arrival to his homestead after his family had died, Jessie recalled that he had behaved with exactly the same kind of distrust and resentment of others.

Reaching the basement, Jessie appreciated the rustic style of decor. Old, rough-cut wooden planks lined the walls. The furniture was of the homemade variety, using large sections of tree trunks as well as branches with some of the bark still remaining to create a very natural and outdoorsy feel to the room. The light fixture hanging from the ceiling in the middle of the room was even decorated with deer antlers, something Jessie himself would have done.

As Jessie stood and admired the room, Jack interrupted his thoughts, saying, "Back here is where you're staying," as he opened a door that was cleverly hidden among the natural gaps between the planks on the wall. No knob or lock was evident to Jessie. It seemed as if Jack merely put his fingers into the wall and made a door simply appear out of nowhere.

"Nice," Jessie said, admiring Jack's handiwork.

"No one but Angela and I know about this, so, well... it had better stay that way," Jack said, his reluctance being apparent.

Following Jack into the room, Jessie looked around to see that the far wall contained heavy-duty, industrial shelving stocked with long-term food storage of various types, as well as two large gun safes along the adjacent, block wall. Several sets of body armor hung from the wall, as well as a decorative display of martial arts swords and other weapons of the craft.

"Impressive," Jessie said.

"I guess you could say Burt Gummer from the movie *Tremors* was my hero," Jack replied. "The guns and ammo are all safely locked away, so I don't have to worry about you getting into that. The other stuff, well, I guess I don't have to worry about that. You've got your own weapons. Plus, if you thought you could take me out with a sword, I'd welcome the attempt. I'm a little rusty and could use the practice."

With a crooked smile, Jessie said, "No… I don't think I will be taking you up on that offer."

"You can sleep here for the night. I'll be back down in the morning. There is a toilet behind that door if you need it," he said, pointing to the wall opposite the gun safes and weapons. "Other than that, stay put. If I find you creeping around my home in the middle of the night, I'll assume the worst. Stay here until I come for you. Is that understood?"

"Yes, sir," Jessie replied with T. R. nodding in agreement.

"Good. The sun will be up soon so you'd better hit the sack. Who knows what kind of day tomorrow will be with all things considered. I feel like a ball has been set into motion that simply can't be stopped. I've kinda had that feeling for the past few days." Shaking himself out of his own thoughts, Jack said, "Well, goodnight," as he turned and left the room, closing the hidden door behind him.

## Chapter Nineteen

Waking to the sounds of several men's voices in the next room, Leina sat up quickly, her heart racing, unsure of where she was and what had happened. Quickly looking around, trying to piece the situation together, she found herself undressed and in a large king-sized bed, alone. Rolling over while throwing the covers to the side, she felt her right leg yank to a stop, finding herself attached to the bed by what seemed to be a set of stainless-steel, law-enforcement-style ankle restraints, similar to handcuffs, but with longer chains. With one end of the restraints locked securely around her ankle, and the other attached to the sturdy wooden frame of the bed, a mix of emotions rushed through her body.

*That son-of-a-b—,* she thought as she had clearly been victimized by Chief Peronne and his men. Her anger quickly turned to heartache and dismay, as she realized that if this was the outcome of her dealings with Chief Peronne, the odds of the children being returned to her were slim to none.

"I'm gonna kill him. I'm gonna kill him. I'm gonna kill that dirty son-of-a-b— if it's the last thing I do," she mumbled through a clenched jaw and gritted teeth.

Her head still swirling from the after-effects of what she could only assume was some sort of drug-induced state, she looked around the room to see her clothes piled in a corner against the far wall and out of her reach. Raising her left leg, she prepared to kick the footboard of the bed in an attempt to break the wood and free herself. She stopped short, though, thinking to herself, *No, they'll hear me. They're just outside the door. I've got to think this through. I've got to be smart about this.*

Laying her head back down on the pillow, she looked at the ceiling, closed her eyes, and began to cry as she thought of the children, whom she now doubted she would ever see again. Thoughts of Kayla, Patricia, and Gavin, raced through her head as a dark, painful sadness began to set in. She now knew that it was Peronne and his men that ambushed their group, killing all but her and the children. Her memories, clouded by drugs and the blow to her head, started to come back into the forefront of her mind.

As she lay there, tortured by her thoughts, the door to the room opened slowly. Her heart began to race, not knowing what would come next. In walked the elderly Hispanic woman called Rosa, who had brought her freshly laundered clothes to the room where she had first been kept. Pulling the covers over her naked body, Leina watched as Rosa quickly walked over to the dresser, placing some of what she assumed was Peronne's clothing into a drawer.

Attempting to avoid making eye contact with Leina, Rosa turned and walked back toward the door. "Wait," Leina murmured. "Don't go. Please," she begged.

Stopping, Rosa turned to look at her with a tear in her eye. "I'm sorry. I can't help you," Rosa said in a defeated tone.

"Please, don't leave me here like this. You know what they are doing to me, and what they will do. Please help me."

"I can't," Rosa replied, looking at the floor in shame.

"These men, they killed my friends. They took my children. I need to get out of here. I need to find my children. You've got to understand."

As tears ran down her face, Rosa walked over to Peronne's wine bar and took something in her hand. Walking over to Leina, she placed a corkscrew on the bed beside her, and quickly turned, running out of the room.

Taking the corkscrew, Leina hid it beneath the covers and closed her eyes, saying a silent prayer for the strength she knew she would need to make it out of her ordeal. *Please, Lord, please help me find a way out of here. Please help me to find the children. I've lost everything to this awful world. My husband Cas, my friends, my children, and now my freedom. Help me, give me the strength...*

Her thoughts were interrupted by the sound of footsteps walking toward the door. Hearing a brief, muffled conversation, she heard a set of footsteps walking away from the room, while the door slowly creaked open. Closing her eyes, pretending to be asleep, Leina listened to what sounded like a man's footsteps, walking slowly across the room to the bed.

Feeling the covers being pulled back, exposing her naked body, she trembled inside as she fought the instinct to react. Feeling a man's hand on her bare breast, she could wait no longer. Leina swung her right hand across her body, opening her eyes to see Officer Barnes standing over her as the corkscrew plunged into his neck.

Grasping the hand that he had placed on her breast with her left, she held him in place while she stabbed him repeatedly in the neck. Blood sprayed all over her, the coils of the corkscrew tearing chunks of flesh free with each violent thrust.

Looking directly into his eyes, seeing sheer terror on his face as his free hand fumbled for his gun, she said, "Enjoy your time in Hell, you son-of-a-b—," as she plunged the corkscrew into the temple of his head, killing him instantly.

His lifeless body collapsing on top of her, the bed becoming soaked with blood, she struggled to reach his belt. Removing his handcuff key, she shoved his body aside, freeing her from his smothering weight. Sitting up and quickly while releasing her restraints, she crawled off the bed and stripped him of his duty belt containing his holstered pistol and spare magazines.

Still naked and now covered with blood, Leina pulled open a drawer containing what she assumed were Chief Peronne's undershirts. Using them as towels, she wiped off as much of

Barnes's blood as she could and began looking around for something to wear. Pulling out drawer after drawer and dumping the contents onto the floor, Leina found a drawer containing sweat pants and workout clothing. Quickly donning both the pants and hooded sweatshirt of a jogging-style suit, she fastened the duty belt around her waist, pulling it to the tightest possible notch, and drew the 9mm Glock from the holster. Checking the action, verifying that a round was in the chamber and that the magazine was fully seated, she tiptoed over to the door, listening for any signs of another officer on the other side.

Running across the room to the west-facing window, she looked outside to see that she was on the second floor, and beneath her was a stone patio. Knowing that jumping from that distance would almost certainly cause a serious injury, especially while barefoot, she slipped back across the room, listening once again for sounds on the other side of the door.

Hearing nothing, she opened the door quietly and looked down the hallway, seeing no one present. Slipping down the hall toward the stairs, she could hear footsteps walking across the old wooden floor downstairs, its creaks giving away the person's position.

Moving silently down the stairway, she could see an officer in the main parlor area of the house, sitting on the sofa with his feet up on the coffee table. With the stairs running down behind the sofa and with the officer's back to her, Leina carefully snuck across the floor behind him and into the kitchen of the home.

Walking over to the knife rack, Leina removed a decorative chef's knife with a Damascus-steel blade and what appeared to be an ivory handle.

Turning her attentions back to the man on the sofa, Leina crept ever so quietly behind him. Slowly reaching out with her left hand, and in an act of vengeance, she grabbed him by the hair, pulled his head back, and slid the blade across his throat, slicing him from ear to ear. As her rage continued to build, she kept sawing violently back and forth until his head detached from his body.

Breathing heavily, with the blood of two men now splattered on her face and in her hair, she looked down at the grizzly scene, turned to look at the front door, then tossed the head onto the floor of the main entryway. Hitting the floor, the head bounced and rolled, leaving a trail of blood behind it before coming to rest on a fancy decorative rug.

Walking over to the large, front-facing windows, Leina pushed the curtain back slightly with the blade of the knife, looking for any signs that the home was being watched.

Seeing a patrol car coming down the street toward the house, Leina ran back into the kitchen and slipped out the back door, disappearing into the surrounding neighborhood.

## Chapter Twenty

Awakened by the sound of the door being opened, Jessie quickly sat up and reached for his Colt. Hearing Jack's voice say, "Relax," it's just me. I brought you some coffee," Jessie took his hand off his gun and breathed a sigh of relief as he realized he had made it through yet another night without any of his ominous nightmares. His days that start out in such a manner never seem to go well for him.

"You have coffee?" Jessie asked in an upbeat tone.

"Yes, although I probably don't want to know where it came from," Jack replied. "I got it through the city as part of our food rations, which is how they pay us these days when we work."

"What time is it?" Jessie asked.

"It's seven-thirty," Jack replied as he began pouring both Jessie and T. R. a cup. Handing a cup to Jessie, Jack said, "The other is for your buddy over there when he wakes up," gesturing toward T. R.

"He's still out cold, huh?" Jessie said. "Well, neither one of us has gotten much rest in the last few days. It felt good to sleep in a semi-secure environment last night. Thanks again for the hospitality."

Changing the subject, Jack said, "Angela is off to work. She's gonna see what she can find out today. When she gets back this evening, we'll take what we have and go from there. For now, you two just need to stay put down here, just in case someone reported seeing you in town. Eyes are everywhere these days. Even without all the high-tech electronic surveillance the government used prior to the collapse, controlling the food supply will get people to do just about anything for you. Being a lookout pays very well, I've heard."

Taking a seat in an old wooden chair, Jack leaned back against the wall and took a sip of coffee. Pointing at Jessie's holster, he said, "What are you doing carrying that old relic around? Haven't you been able to find an upgrade somewhere after all of this time?"

"This old relic is all I have left of my past," Jessie said as he slid the gun out of its holster. Looking it over with fondness, he explained, "My father was a sheriff's deputy when I was a boy. He carried this same pistol, and it saved his life more than once. Then, later in life, when I entered a law enforcement career myself, he handed it down to me. He died shortly after that, and well, I just wouldn't part with this thing for the world, now. It's saved my butt more times than I can count. It's old and weathered, it's hardly got any finish left, and it's scuffed up pretty bad, but to me, it's a work of art. No, there is no upgrade from this gun. It's perfect just the way it is."

Sliding the gun back into its holster, Jessie took a sip of coffee as Jack said, "So, you were a sheriff in Colorado?"

"Yeah, Montezuma County. Before the collapse, that is. My last election didn't go so well. My opponent had money and connections. To say that I think the vote count was rigged would be a waste of breath. There toward the end, it seemed like all elections were frauds. The people selected by the elites to be put into power always seemed to come up with the necessary vote count in the end."

"Tell me about it. Hell, at least we had elections back then, even if they were rigged. Peronne has never been elected, and that bastard is dominating the entire town."

"That needs to change," Jessie said, taking another sip.

"It will. Trust me," Jack replied.

Kicking T. R.'s cot, Jessie said, "Time to get up. Your coffee is getting cold."

With a yawn and a stretch, T. R. looked around the room, rubbed his eyes, and said, "Man, I must have slept like the dead last night."

"Don't get used to it," Jack replied sharply, changing the tone of the conversation.

Hearing the door open upstairs, Jack quickly stood up as he heard Angela's voice yelling, "Daddy! Daddy!"

Running out of the room and up the stairs, followed by both Jessie and T. R., Jack found Angela rushing to meet him.

"What? What is it? What happened?" he asked.

Stopping to catch her breath, she replied, "Something went down last night at Peronne's home."

"What?"

"I'm not exactly sure, but I know that two of his officers are dead. And Rosa, Peronne's maid, they raided her home and dragged her out kicking and screaming. Peronne is on the warpath, too. I heard him yelling that he was gonna tear the town apart looking for her."

"Who?"

"I don't know. At that point, one of his men cleared us all out of City Hall and sent us all home for the day."

"Could it be the woman they were keeping?" Jessie asked.

"I... I don't know," she replied. "That's the first thing I thought of, though."

"Well, guys," Jack said, turning to Jessie and T. R., "if something is gonna happen, it's gonna be soon. Peronne isn't gonna let this go. He can't let his department take a hit like that without making it clear to everyone in town that he still has an iron grip on everything. The last thing a wannabe dictator wants to do is show any signs of weakness or vulnerability. No, I would venture to guess that if Rosa had anything to do with what happened at his home, he'll come down on her and her family hard."

"So, what do we do?" asked Jessie.

Looking at T. R., Jack asked, "What's the situation at the jail? Is that where they would have taken her?"

"More than likely," T. R. replied. "The jail is inside the De Baca County Courthouse. If they are after someone, though, especially after the loss of four of their men over the past few days, the courthouse will have minimal staffing. They'll double up on patrols, and probably start a door-to-door search. It won't be pretty, either. It will be just as much an exhibition of power and control as it is about finding whoever it is they are looking for."

Looking back at Jack, Jessie said, "Look, we don't know what's going on with the limited information that we have, but it would seem that this is a moment of opportunity. If Peronne and his men have their attention turned elsewhere, we can use the chaos of the situation to make a move."

Scratching his chin, Jack asked, "What do you suggest?"

"I came here with the intention of finding out what happened to the children that were taken in the ambush east of town. That's still my priority. Without intel, though, we're just gonna be randomly fighting Peronne's men with no clear objective. I think we need to get our hands on that Rosa woman. If she betrayed Peronne and helped the woman they were holding escape, then her allegiances have been broken, and she has nothing left to lose. Being his personal maid, she probably knows more about what goes on behind the scenes than anyone outside of the police department."

"That makes sense," Jack replied.

Angela added, "Rosa is a wonderful woman. We've got to help her, intel or not. But I agree, she's probably the best source of information we've got. She had access to places no one else in town, other than Peronne's men, could go."

Looking at T. R., Jessie said, “Can you get us in? You know the facility, right?”

“I know the layout and the security protocols, but it’s a relatively secure building. It’s an old building. Very sturdy and well built. The lower level is all thick masonry with steel covers over the windows. The upper levels are brick, several feet thick, I would guess. The doors are reinforced with steel, and the windows are all barred between the panes of glass, it looks decorative, but they’re tough.”

Picking up a pen and a piece of scrap paper, Jack handed it to T. R., and said, “Draw the basic layout. Where might they be keeping her?”

Taking the pen in hand, T. R. began to sketch out the basic floorplan of the building to the best of his knowledge, saying, “The main entry is up the steps on the second level. The holding cells are in the basement. Like I said, the windows to the basement are covered with large steel plates.”

Taking the paper in hand and studying it for a moment, Jack placed it back on the table, put his finger on the drawing, and said, “Where, in here, would she likely be?”

“Probably in one of these, but that’s just a guess,” he said, marking the paper as he spoke.

“Alright, then. I’ve got to meet with a few people and work a few things out,” said Jack as he folded the paper and put it into his shirt pocket. “You two be working your way to the courthouse. I want you to both find a position on the east side of the building. When I arrive, make your move.”

“What? Um, make our move? What do you mean?” Jessie asked, confused.

“Like I said, I’ve got to work a few things out,” Jack explained. You’ll know when I’m there. And you’ll know when it’s time. Once we are able to make entry into the building, follow my lead.”

Looking at T. R., seeing the same look of confusion on his face, Jessie shrugged and said, “Roger that. But how will you know where we are?”

“I’ll see you when the shooting starts. Don’t worry, it will all be obvious. Besides, thinking we’re gonna be sticking to some sort of well-developed plan is a fantasy anyway. We’ve got to move now and on very little information. This is a shoot-from-the-hip type operation at best. Just roll with it,” Jack said confidently as he put on his jacket and gave Angela a kiss on the cheek. “Angela, you come with me. We’ll see you boys there.”

As Jack and Angela rushed out of the home, Jessie and T. R. looked at each other with mutual expressions of confusion. Shrugging his shoulders, Jessie said, “You heard the man. Let’s get back downstairs and get loaded up.”

## Chapter Twenty-One

Working their way through town, moving skillfully from street to street, Jessie and T. R. covered each other as they moved in bounds. Along the way, they encountered Peronne's men at several locations as they searched homes all throughout the town. Arriving just across Avenue C from the courthouse, T. R. and Jessie took shelter in an abandoned block and stucco automotive garage that was in the parking lot of a former Valero gas station. Looking through the small windows in the roll-up door, they could see the courthouse as well as one of the desert-tan SUV's. Noting the lack of movement outside the courthouse, Jessie said, "And now we wait."

"I wonder what Jack has in mind," T. R. thought aloud.

"Yeah, same here. I'm not sure if he didn't want to tell us for OPSEC reasons, or if he just had yet to figure it out himself. One thing is for sure, though."

"What's that?" T. R. asked.

"We've got a good idea of who is in Peronne's back pocket, now."

"How?"

"Didn't you notice? Along the way, every time we encountered Peronne's men kicking doors while looking for whoever it is they're looking for, they didn't hit every house. They skipped some for no apparent reason. Odds are, those houses are the eyes and ears."

"Yeah, Good point," T. R. replied, agreeing with Jessie's deductions.

Sitting down on the floor and leaning against the wall in the darkest corner of the room, Jessie said, "You've got first watch."

"Come again?" T. R. queried.

Lifting his hat to look T. R. in the eye, Jessie said, "Look, we don't know how long it's gonna take for anything to begin, much less to play out. We've got to assume we're gonna be here for a while, and then whenever it does all hit the fan, that it will take some time to play out. When the situation before you is full of variables and unknowns, you've got to proactively manage the knowns. With that in mind, I'm gonna manage a nap. Wake me in two hours unless you feel the need to prior to that, then I'll take a shift by the window."

Shaking his head with a grin, T. R. said, "Roger that, Sheriff."

Looking back up at T. R., Jessie said, "I wish you could still call me that. Just call me Jessie. There's no sense in dwelling on the past. Hell, there's barely a future to dwell on."

With a nod, T. R. turned and looked back out the window, watching the only movement he could see, that of a gentle breeze blowing an old plastic shopping bag down the street. *I wonder how long that thing has been aimlessly wandering the world.*

~~~~

Riding Brave back to the homestead at a leisurely trot, Jessie could see the smoke emanating from the chimney of the cabin over the next hill. Seeing the smoke from the chimney always made Jessie smile as he returned home. He knew the smoke meant that the cabin was nice and cozy inside, and Stephanie no doubt had something delicious cooking on top of the wood stove.

As Jessie rounded the last bend, he looked around in amazement at the beauty of their mountain retreat, and counted their many blessings. Looking back at his bounty stretched across the back of his saddle, Jessie counted them and said to
~~~~

himself aloud, "Four rabbits and three squirrels. That'll make a nice change of pace from lamb and mutton."

Refocusing on the cabin up ahead, now clearly visible, Jessie noticed that both the front screen door and wooden doors had been left standing wide open. Feeling concerned, knowing that Stephanie's pet peeve was to keep the bugs out and the heat in, he nudged Brave forward, increasing his pace.

Arriving at the front of the cabin, Jessie quickly climbed down from Brave, tied his reins to the porch railing, and went inside. Looking around the room, seeing a fresh batch of homemade biscuits on the table and the teapot boiling over on the stove, Jessie said, "Steph? Sasha? Jeremy? Where are you?"

Walking over the to the bedroom door, Jessie turned the knob and swung it open. To his horror, he saw his beloved family, his beautiful wife, Stephanie, and his loving children, Sasha and Jeremy, all lying on the bed, piled one on top of another, with their throats slashed from ear to ear. The white bedsheets that Jessie and Stephanie had slept on for years, were now soaked with their blood, as it dripped down onto the floor below.

Before he could react, a hand reached from behind the door, grasping him by the throat with a raspy voice saying, "Well, well... Daddy is finally home. Looks like you're a little too late, Daddy," the voice said with a dark chuckle as the greasy, unkempt, and rotten-toothed man emerged into Jessie's view. The smell of body odor and foul, rotten breath overwhelmed him.

Reaching for his Colt in a fit of absolute rage, Jessie yelled, "You, son-of-a-b—!" as he cocked the hammer with his thumb while shoving the barrel into the man's forehead.

"Jessie! No! It's me!" T. R. said sheepishly as he watched the cylinder of the old Colt rotate as Jessie's thumb pulled the hammer back into the cocked position. Looking into Jessie's eyes and seeing the rage of a madman, he once again said, "It's me... it's me, man. It's your turn. That's all."

His eyes regaining their focus, Jessie felt his finger begin to apply pressure on the trigger as he saw T. R.'s face come into view. Quickly pulling the gun off T. R.'s forehead. Jessie could see him shivering with fear. Looking around the room, regaining his composure and collecting his thoughts, Jessie said, "Sorry," as he wiped a tear from his eye.

"Hey, man, are you okay?" T. R. asked.

"Yeah. Yeah, I'm all right," Jessie said as he attempted to shrug off his emotions. The dream feeling so real to him, both the love of his family and the memories of his tragic loss sending his mind into a dark and violent spiral. "What, what is it?"

"You said to wake you in two hours," T. R. replied. "It's that time. I just came over to wake you. Sorry if I startled you."

"Have you ever felt like you had finally moved on from something, releasing the pain, only to have it haunt you and pierce your heart yet again? I guess clinging to the pain can be a good thing," Jessie added as he avoided eye contact with T. R. "Pain reminds you of reality. In this world, it's good to keep the reality of things right in front of you. There's no room for weakness here. None at all. Weakness is how people like Peronne gain power over the rest of us. How many tragedies has Peronne caused? How many families have lost loved ones? How many children were taken? No, there's no room for weakness, here."

Standing up and dusting himself off, Jessie said, "Enough of that. Get some sleep while you still can," as he walked over to the small, oval window on the garage door, taking his post for the next two hours.

As T. R. lay in the darkest corner of the room attempting to fall asleep, Jessie gazed out the small, dirty window, seeing only the movement of the tree branches as they blew with the gentle breeze. The courthouse itself sat back from the road approximately fifty yards on the other side of Avenue C, with its decorative trees and shrubbery being overgrown to the point that details of the building itself were hard to see.

After about a half-hour, Jessie heard T. R. snort and begin to snore. *Finally, he's asleep,* he thought as he looked over to see T. R.'s hat over his face, with his arm behind his head for a pillow. Hearing the sound of a vehicle approaching from the west to the east down Avenue C, Jessie's attention was once again directed out the garage door window as he watched one of the desert tan painted SUV's arrive in front of the courthouse, now making two vehicles total.

Observing for several minutes, he saw two officers exit the courthouse, climb into the first SUV, and drive away, heading back to the west from where the second vehicle came. Looking at his watch, Jessie wondered to himself, *shift change?*

After approximately ten more minutes of watching and waiting, Jessie heard a rumble from the east. Picking up an old, empty oil bottle, he tossed it at T. R., striking him on the leg, startling him awake. T. R. quickly sat up, reached for his rifle, and said, "Wha... what? What is it?"

"Something's up," Jessie said, staring out the window. "Something big is headed this way."

Scurrying to his feet, T. R. joined Jessie by the window and began nervously looking about. Unable to see adequately to the east from the small window, Jessie whispered, "Sounds like a big diesel engine to me." Pausing to listen more carefully, he added, "Tracks."

"What?" T. R. asked, seeking clarification of Jessie's statement.

"It's a tracked vehicle. Peronne doesn't have tanks, too, does he?" Jessie asked sarcastically.

"No, just regular street vehicles," replied T. R.

As the squeaks, clacks, and moans of metallic tracks and a diesel engine drew near, an old, rust-covered Caterpillar D5 dozer came into view. “Holy hell,” Jessie said. “Is that Jack?”

“Sure looks like it,” T. R. replied.

“Better get ready. It looks like the show is about to start.”

As the dozer passed in front of the garage, Jack pulled back hard on the right steering lever, locking up the right track and sharply pivoting the dozer to turn to the right. He then opened up the throttle, lowered the blade slightly, and angled the six-way blade all the way to the left, exposing the right corner of the large, U-shaped blade.

Adjusting his path and blade height, Jack aimed the corner of the angled blade at one of the lower, steel-covered basement windows. Just as bullets began bouncing off of the dozer from a window on the main floor of the building, he jumped free of the machine and dove behind one of the trees on the courthouse lawn for cover.

Just as Jessie started to say something, he noticed the impact of bullets striking the courthouse as if to provide cover for Jack, as he would otherwise be pinned down and alone on the courthouse lawn.

“He’s not alone,” Jessie said, “Let’s go.”

With a nod in the affirmative, Jessie and T. R. watched as the corner of the dozer blade struck the steel-reinforced basement window, shattering the block foundation, knocking the large, steel plates into the basement. The dozer, now unmanned with its diesel engine still running, began to churn its tracks into the dirt, now firmly up against the immoveable, thick masonry foundation of the nearly one-hundred-year-old structure.

Rushing across the street, Jessie made his way to the police SUV parked alongside Avenue C. Once in position, he motioned for T. R. to rally on him as someone continued to pound the courthouse with a high powered rifle from afar, keeping the shooter on the main floor of the building at bay. Joining Jessie behind the SUV, T. R. said, "What's the plan?"

"We've gotta move quick," Jessie shouted over the gunfire and the sound of the still roaring diesel engine. "Backup should be here anytime. We need to make entry before they get here and shoot us in the back while doing so. We'll never make it inside taking fire from both directions."

"I can start this thing," T. R. said, referring to the desert tan Chevy Suburban SUV. "There is always an extra key in the ashtray for emergencies."

"Check it out," Jessie said as he looked to Jack's position.

Climbing inside the Suburban from the passenger's side door, T. R. fumbled around, finding the key while keeping his head down low. He shoved the key into the ignition from across the vehicle, turned it, and the engine came to life. Slipping back out of the Suburban, he motioned for Jessie to join him as they both climbed inside.

Signaling to Jack, it appeared as if Jack relayed what was going on to someone via a small, hand-held radio.

"Put this thing between Jack and the building," Jessie shouted. "Then get the hell out and up against the wall so that the main floor shooter can't get a line on you without exposing himself to our guardian angel. That'll give Jack cover so that he can make a move as well."

"Roger that!" T. R. said as he put the Suburban into gear, released the parking brake, and began speeding toward the building, bouncing over the curb and tearing across the grass toward Jack.

Arriving at Jack's position, Jessie slipped out the passenger's side door and moved alongside the rear of the SUV, joining up with Jack. As T. R. made a run for the masonry foundation of the building, Jessie said, "It's about time you got here," shouting over the sound of the dozer.

"I was thinking the same thing," Jack replied. "If you guys hadn't made it here, I'd be screwed when their backup arrives. Speaking of which, there they come," he said, pointing toward the west as another SUV sped toward them from a distance.

"Cover. Moving," Jack said into the radio as the cadence of long-range fire on the building intensified, allowing both him and Jessie the opportunity to make their move, joining T. R. alongside the foundation of the building.

Patting T. R. on the shoulder, Jessie pointed toward the approaching SUV and shouted, "No time. Gotta move. Cover our entrance, then follow."

With a nod in the affirmative, T. R. worked his way to the dozer's blade as the tracks churned ominously into the dirt, the blade still wedged firmly into the large window opening with the steel shutters dangling from their damaged hinges. T. R. couldn't help but think of how bad the timing would be if the dozer suddenly found traction as they worked their way through the opening. *Thank God this concrete foundation is several feet thick*, he thought.

Seeing T. R. nod to him that he was ready, Jessie said, "Let's go!" as he and Jack made their move.

Firing a few shots inside to clear the way, T. R. turned his attention to the approaching SUV that slid sideways as it made an aggressive turn onto the courthouse lawn, barreling toward them at a high rate of speed. Opening fire on the SUV's windshield with his AR-15, focusing on the driver's side, but spreading his shots across the entire width of the windshield, the SUV slid to a stop as return fire began to erupt through the shattered safety glass. As the high-speed projectiles began exploding off the masonry foundation all around him, T. R. felt a tug on his leg as Jessie urged him inside. Turning and diving into the window, T. R. narrowly avoided a barrage of bullets that peppered the location where he had crouched only seconds before.

"What do we have?" T. R. asked.

"Nothing yet," Jessie replied. "If there is a minimum of two officers in the building, we have to assume the shooter is still above us on the main floor. If Rosa is being held down here in the basement, like you said, the other is probably down here."

Jack spoke up and said, "Look, he knows the building best," gesturing toward T. R. while talking directly to Jessie. "Take him with you to clear the way. I'll keep our buddies on the lawn at bay as best I can."

Turning to fire out of the basement window, Jack emptied the remaining contents of his AR15's thirty-round magazine into the disabled SUV, momentarily halting the return fire. With his shots keeping the occupants of the vehicle at bay, Jessie and T. R. began working their way down the dark hallway, illuminated only by the light shining through the opening made by the dozer.

Motioning for T. R. to take the point position, Jessie held his AR-10 at the high ready position, while following T. R. down the left side of the hallway.

With barely enough light to see in the dark and musty basement, with even the slightest sound echoing off the thick concrete walls, T. R. motioned for Jessie to hold his position as they approached a door on the left side of the hallway. Hearing Jack shout, "Hurry up, guys!" from down the hallway, T. R. reached out to the lever-style doorknob, rotated it downward, and pushed the door open as it swung to the inside of the room. His heart raced as he quickly reaffirmed his grip on his AR15.

Taking a deep breath, T. R. stepped out from the wall and sliced-the-pie around the corner of the door, looking through the sights of his rifle as he checked for threats in the room.

Stepping back toward the wall, he signaled to Jessie that he was unsure of the situation. "It's too dark," he whispered.

"Gotta clear it," Jessie responded. "If we keep working our way down the hall, and someone is in there, we could get shot in the back. You're gonna have to suck it up and make entry. I'd rather risk getting shot in the front while my sights are on target than risk getting shot in the back. You go low and I'll go high. On my signal."

Nodding that he understood, T. R. took another deep breath, crouched down with his rifle at the low ready and waited for Jessie's signal. Feeling a pat on his shoulder, he rushed into the room with Jessie following close behind.

Entering the room tucked in tight behind T. R., Jessie flipped on his weapon-mounted flashlight and quickly scanned the room, momentarily extinguishing it while changing his position. Flicking it back on and scanning the room once again, he saw what appeared to be rows of metal shelving containing old, archived court documents and other such administrative materials. After searching each row of shelving, Jessie motioned for T. R. to continue down the hallway.

~~~~

As Jack worked to keep the officers in the SUV at bay, he saw two more vehicles approaching at high rates of speed from both the east and the west. *Ah, hell...* he thought, knowing he was about to be outgunned, even with his position of cover. "Hurry up, guys!" he shouted.

Seeing one of the SUV's stop just shy of the courthouse, he watched as it changed direction and drove around behind the building via a side street. The other SUV then made a run for the men he had been holding back with suppressing fire. Turning his attention to the charging vehicle, Jack began to receive fire
~~~~

from his previous targets of interest, forcing him to take cover below the masonry foundation of the building.

Taking a quick glance and then ducking back behind cover, he noticed the men had now joined up, and were advancing on his position using bulletproof SWAT-style shields to make their move on the building. Checking his small, sling-style pack, Jack realized that with only two magazines of ammunition remaining, he couldn't maintain an effective resistance much longer.

Just then, one of the men advancing on him fell forward with a sudden impact, causing the others to scatter as they realized they were facing a threat to their rear as well. Taking only a few steps, a second man fell face down to the ground, lifeless, taking a direct hit in the back while the other two of the four escaped, running out of sight and around the building.

*That's my girl,* Jack thought to himself with a smile.

~~~~

Having worked their way down the dark hallway, clearing each room as they went, Jessie and T. R. arrived at the final door at the end of the hall. Quietly creeping up to the door, Jessie put his finger to his lips to signal T. R. to remain silent while he attempted to listen for any signs that the room was occupied.

Unable to hear anything coming from the room, Jessie communicated his intentions to T. R. with a simple nod as he reached for the handle. *Damn it,* he thought, realizing the door was locked.

Feeling around the door in the near total darkness, not wanting to give himself away with his light just yet, Jessie determined that like the others, the door opened to the inside, swinging inward and to the right. Motioning for T. R. to follow, the two men slipped back down the hallway and entered one of the previously cleared rooms.
~~~~

"What's the plan?" T. R. whispered.

Ignoring him for a moment while he looked around the room for something of use, Jessie hurried over to a large, metal storage shelf on castering wheels, and said, "This thing weighs a ton. It'll do," as he began to push it toward the door leading to the hallway.

"Battering ram?" T. R. queried.

"Yep," Jessie replied. "If we can't sneak in, we'll have to make a slightly more dramatic entry. Once we get into the room, I'll break left, and you break right, each of us covering our respective sides of the room. If you've got a better idea, speak up now. We've got no time to mess around, though. Jack can't hold them off forever."

"Roger that," T. R. replied as the two men pushed the paper and office supply laden shelf on wheels into the hallway.

Reaching the center of the hall, Jessie looked at T. R. and said, "Here goes. If the door doesn't open, this is gonna hurt."

With that, the two men began pushing the heavy cart, getting off to a slow start at first, with speed and momentum building as they ran behind it, pushing from both sides. With their speed now up to a jog, Jessie and T. R. braced themselves as they reached the door, smashing it off its hinges, violently entering the room.

Flicking on their weapon-mounted lights, Jessie and T. R. dove to each side, scanning the room for threats. Hearing a woman's scream, Jessie looked to the corner, where he saw the woman he assumed to be Rosa, gagged and handcuffed, sitting on the floor with fear in her eyes.

"It's okay," Jessie said as he reached out with his hand to comfort her. Staring into her eyes, he could see that her gaze was transfixed on something behind him.

Almost immediately, Jessie heard the concussion of a rifle blast, followed by a flash of light and an impact knocking him forward to the floor.

Disoriented, Jessie felt the weight of a man on top of him, along with a warm, wet sensation soaking through his clothes.

"Jessie!" T. R. shouted as he ran to his side, pulling the body of one of Peronne's men off him.

Quickly rolling over, Jessie's heart raced as he came to his senses, realizing that T. R. had shot a threat that was hiding in the shadows, the body falling into Jessie and knocking him to the ground.

With their ears ringing from the supersonic crack of T. R.'s 5.56 NATO round being discharged in the confines of the small, basement room, Jessie ran to the woman's side as he heard T. R. say, "It's her. It's Rosa," through the pain and ringing in his ears.

"Keys?" Jessie shouted, turning to look at T. R.

Reaching into his pocket and kneeling down beside Rosa, T. R. unlocked the handcuffs and removed the gag from around her mouth. Looking at T. R. in fear and confusion, recognizing him as one of Peronne's men, Rosa started to scream as T. R. held his hands up and said, "It's okay. It's okay. I'm not with them anymore. We came to get you out of here."

Looking at Jessie and then back to T. R., Rosa reluctantly took T. R.'s hand and stood up, trusting what he said for the moment.

~~~~

Scanning the area surrounding the courthouse from his limited perspective in the basement, seeing no other signs of Peronne's men, Jack's attention momentarily drifted to the churning tracks of the dozer just before him. Looking around at the structure, he thought to himself, *I'm not sure whether it's*
~~~~

*the strength of this old masonry building or the soft layer of decorative topsoil around it stealing that dozer's traction, but I'm sure glad it's holding up,* as he reached up and pounded his fist on the dozer's blade that was wedged firmly into the opening.

Continuing to stay vigilant, Jack quickly looked down the darkened hallway for any signs of Jessie or T. R., but saw nothing. Quickly turning back toward the exterior of the building, Jack's eyes latched onto the bottom of the dozer's tracks as they churned away at what was his eye level from his perspective in the basement. *Damn, I wish I could climb up there and shut that thing off,* he thought. *Sitting here underneath a bulldozer that's trying it's best to run straight through you is a tad bit unnerving.*

Picking up his radio, Jack pressed the transmit button, and said, "Hangin' in there?"

A reply quickly came over the radio in a female voice, nearly lost in the garble of static, "Yep."

"Nice work," he replied with a smile.

"I learned from the best," the female voice again replied.

"Just hang tight a little longer."

"Will do," she replied.

Clipping his radio back onto his belt, Jack looked up at the dozer's churning tracks that seemed almost hypnotic by this point, and detected a slight bit of movement. His heart skipping a beat, Jack immediately looked up and noticed a large crack starting to form in the building's old stone foundation. "Crap!" he said aloud as his eyes focused on the churning tracks. "That son-of-a-b— has dug its way down to rock," as the dozer's diesel engine took on a noticeable load, finding traction beneath the soil.

Unable to hear the sound of the cracking foundation over the roar of the still-running diesel engine, Jack turned to run as he began to see the light fade from behind him as the dozer started pushing through the foundation, falling into the basement compartment, coming to a stop only when the floor overhead came crashing down on top of it with the blade digging itself firmly into the stone floor below.

Stunned and disoriented, dusting himself off, coughing the old, musty rock dust out of his lungs, only to choke once again from the inhalation of diesel exhaust fumes that were now being pumped directly into the basement from the roaring engine, Jack attempted to stand up, only to realize that he was trapped. Unable to escape the collapsing wall in time, Jack's leg was pinned beneath a pile of rubble. Looking off to his right, he saw the blade of the dozer buried deep into the floor, only inches from him. *Damn, that was close,* he thought as he struggled to free his trapped legs, only to feel a sharp and excruciating pain shoot through his body causing him to scream aloud.

~~~~

Hearing a loud crash from down the hallway, followed by Jack's pain-filled scream, Jessie turned to T. R. and said, "Stay with her. I'll be back."

Running down the hall with his AR-10 at the high ready and his weapon-mounted light now lighting his way in the dark hallway, Jessie began to cough from the diesel exhaust fumes that rapidly filled the poorly ventilated basement hallway. Seeing the dozer just up ahead atop a pile of rubble, Jessie saw Jack lying face down, partially covered in crumbled concrete, stones, and mortar.

"Jack! Are you okay?" Jessie shouted over the loud roar of the engine and the mechanical noise made by the still-churning tracks.
~~~~

Giving him a thumbs-up, Jack coughed again and shouted, "Shut that thing off!"

Looking at the moving tracks and the precarious angle at which the dozer sat, Jessie realized that simply climbing into the operator's seat to shut the machine off would not be as easy as it might seem. Thinking quickly, he opened the engine compartment's side-access door, located the diesel engine's injection pump, followed the fuel-inlet line, and found a manual fuel shut-off valve, closing it, bringing the roaring engine and clanging tracks to a stop.

"Are you okay?" he asked again, kneeling down by Jack's side.

"My leg," Jack said in a short and stress-filled manner. "I think it's broken. I tried to get it free, but couldn't."

Resting his rifle against the dozer in a position to shine his weapon-mounted light on the pile of rubble, Jessie said, "Keep an eye on things down the hallway. T. R. is with Rosa, so don't shoot them by mistake."

"You found her? Good!" Jack replied. "Is she okay?"

"She seemed fine to me," said Jessie as he began digging through the rubble.

Tossing a large chunk of concrete to the side, Jessie asked, "So, what happened? What's our situation outside?"

"I only saw two vehicles approach," Jack replied. "Two of Peronne's men were in each. Two are down hard, and two got away around behind the building. They could be making entry on the level above us by now."

"You got two of them?" Jessie asked.

"Nope. But Angela did."

"Angela?" Jessie queried.

"Yes, Angela. Who do you think was providing over-watch?" Jack answered. "That girl is a hell of a shot. She's been into long-range competitive shooting for years. It was a way for me to get her prepared without actually talking with her mother about what was on my mind about what I saw going on around us."

"Smart man," Jessie replied. "Is she okay out there?"

"I think so. They didn't seem to know where the shots were coming from." Reaching for his belt, Jack retrieved his radio, placed it up to his head, keyed the mic, and said, "Are you there?"

Releasing the transmit button, Jack listened as nothing but static emanated from the radio.

Looking at Jack as he tossed another chunk of concrete aside, Jessie said, "It's probably just that you can't pick her signal up down here. You practically had a line-of-sight on her before."

Coughing and wincing in pain, Jack said, "Yeah, I hope you're right."

## Chapter Twenty-Two

Climbing over a backyard fence and quickly hiding behind what was once a neatly arranged hedgerow, Leina sat on the ground as she inspected her bare feet and thought, *I've got to find some shoes and soon,* as she picked a thorn from her heel. Watching a police SUV speed by, toward the east end of town, she remained hidden for a moment, only to turn and look at the window behind her, with the gap in the curtains being quickly drawn shut.

*Damn it!* she thought, realizing that she was being watched. As she stood in a hunched-over position and plotted her next move, another SUV approached from the east to the west. This time, however, it was moving slowly while an officer on foot on each side of the SUV searched the surrounding areas.

Hearing footsteps behind her, Leina quickly turned, drawing the Glock 9mm from the loose-fitting police duty belt around her waist, only to hear an elderly woman's voice say, "Come inside. Quickly."

Hesitating for a moment, Leina looked at the woman, whom she assumed to be in her early to mid-seventies, wearing a bathrobe with a hairnet and slippers. Lowering the pistol, she began to speak as the woman interrupted her, whispering, "Come on. There's no time to argue."

Holstering the weapon, Leina followed the woman around the side of the house to the back entrance, where a young man in his mid-twenties ushered them inside, closing the door securely behind them.

Rushing to the front of the home, the young man looked through the curtains and said, "Only one house to go. Hurry up."

Taking Leina by the hand, the elderly woman said, "This way, dear. There's no time for discussion. I don't know who you are or what your story is, but it doesn't matter at the moment. We can catch up later."

Leading her into the restroom at the end of the bedroom hallway, the lady opened the closet door, removed a clothes hamper full of used towels, and opened what appeared to Leina to be a hidden door covered with linoleum flooring to match the rest of the room.

"It's cramped, but it's the best we can do for now. Once they're gone, we'll get you out and catch up on whatever is going on. Tommy and I will take care of things up here. If they come in the house, don't worry. They search our homes all the time. We're used to it. Just keep quiet and you'll be fine."

Nodding in reply, Leina slipped into the cramped compartment underneath the floor as the woman replaced the section of flooring overhead, leaving Leina in total darkness.

Hearing the closet door close as the woman left the room, Leina felt around the small, cramped space, which, from what she could tell, measured only four feet by four feet at the most. The space seemed to be very crudely constructed, with moisture seeping through the wood-plank floor.

Feeling a long wooden box off to one side, Leina opened it and felt around inside. *A hunting rifle,* she thought as her fingers traced over what felt to her to be a wooden-stocked, bolt-action rifle with a scope mounted on top. Continuing to explore the contents of the box in the darkness, Leina felt what she thought were several boxes of ammunition and other related supplies.

With nothing but the sounds above her to guide her thoughts, Leina closed her eyes and listened intently as she heard what sounded like one of the main entry doors upstairs being smashed open, followed by the sound of screams from the woman who had helped her hide.

"What are you doing? What's going on?" the woman shouted, followed by the sounds of a physical struggle.

"Leave him alone! Leave Tommy alone!" she yelled with fear in her voice.

"Where is she?" an authoritative man's voice answered. "Where is the woman?"

"What woman, what are you talking about?" she cried.

"Don't play dumb with me," the man's voice shouted. "Where is she? She's a cop killer, and if you're harboring her, that makes you guilty as well."

The voice of a young man whom she assumed to be Tommy replied, "We don't know what you're talking about. There's no one here."

"That's not what your neighbor said. Now, speak up while you still can."

"Leave him alone!" the elderly woman shouted.

Hearing only the sounds of a muted struggle for the next moment, the elderly woman screamed in horror, "Nooooooo!" as the sound of a gunshot rang out, followed by her tearful sobs.

"You bastards! You killed him! You killed him," she cried. "He's all I had left in this world," she cried out in agony.

The woman's sorrowful cries were interrupted by the sounds of an intensified struggle, as it appeared the woman was being dragged from room to room as each door was being kicked open. With the sounds seeming to be growing nearer, the bathroom door above came crashing inward as the woman was thrown against the bathtub, now laying on the floor, crying.

"Where is she?" the man's voice demanded as the cadence of her sobs were interrupted by the sound of deep, sickening thuds as he beat her.

Unable to remain hidden any longer with what was going on above her, Leina quietly pushed up on the hidden door above her. Feeling the weight of the clothes hamper, she moved ever so slowly in an effort to keep the hamper from sliding off the door too quickly, making a noise.

Propping the door open with a mop bucket, Leina slipped from underneath the floor and quietly positioned herself by the closet door. Hearing the woman's whimpers begin to fade, Leina knew she could not wait any longer. Slowly turning the knob to release the bolt from its catch, she gripped the handle of the butcher knife she had taken from Peronne's home and exploded from the closet like a mad woman. She began stabbing the man in the back, piercing his lung as he stood with his hand in the air, poised for another strike at the poor, defenseless woman who now lay in the tub covered in blood.

As the man dropped to his knees, the sounds of gurgling air rushing from his wound as his lung deflated and collapsed, Leina whispered in his ear, "Shhhhh, don't go to hell screaming. You don't want to draw attention to yourself down there."

Pulling the knife from his back, she drew the blade across his throat, spilling his blood on the bathroom floor. Lowering him to the floor slowly by holding onto his hair in order to keep from making any unnecessary sounds, she heard the man's partner coming down the hallway yelling, "Jose! What's going on?"

Entering the room, the man saw his partner lying in a pool of blood on the white linoleum floor, and then, from behind the door, he saw the blade of a large butcher knife come at him as it sliced him across the face, taking the sight from his left eye as Leina tackled him, pushing him into the wall behind him. As he looked down at her rage-filled face, she thrust the knife into his gut. Grabbing his right hand with her left, Leina kept his holstered pistol in place while she repeatedly stabbed him in the stomach with the knife while staring directly into his remaining eye as it filled with blood from the devastating wound.

"You're gonna join your friend in hell real soon, you son-of-a-b—," as she drew the knife across his stomach with a vengeance, spilling his guts onto the floor.

Collapsing into the pile of his own entrails, the man's world faded into darkness as he convulsed in pain. As his final thoughts raced through his mind, knowing that the end was upon him, he saw the faces of all those he had caused to suffer, their eyes staring at him as if they were awaiting their vengeance on the other side.

## Chapter Twenty-Three

"It's us!" Jessie shouted as he kicked the door open, carrying Jack into the room where T. R. had been looking after Rosa.

"What happened?" T. R. said with excitement as he rushed over to help Jessie lay him on a large foldout table.

Cutting through Jack's pant leg with his knife, Jessie said, "The dozer finally worked its way into the basement."

"Got bit by my own attack dog," Jack said, attempting to joke through the pain.

Rushing over to the table to see if she could be of assistance, Rosa wiped the sweat and dirt from Jack's forehead as Jack said, "Damn, Rosa. They worked you over good," noticing the bruising on her face and arms. "I'm so sorry that we didn't do something sooner."

"It's not your fault, Jack. It's mine," she said, looking down at the floor in shame. "I shouldn't have served that tyrant as long as I did."

Taking her by the hand, Jack looked her in the eye and said, "None of us should have let this go on for as long as we did. It's not your fault. We all share the burden of responsibility, but the only ones who can actually share the blame are those out there carrying weapons against us in his name at this very moment."

"But I knew more than most," she said with a tear in her eye. "That's why I had to help the woman. I just couldn't take it anymore. That's why they came for me."

"Woman, what woman?" Jessie asked.

"They brought her in following one of their supply runs to the east of town. I've seen it before. They've never brought men in, from whatever it was they were doing out there, only women, and only attractive ones at that."

"What do you know about her?" he asked.

"She was a strong one. Her only weakness seemed to be for her children. She asked for them repeatedly, but Peronne and his men kept telling her they were being looked after and cared for at the clinic, which I know was not true. They just kept stalling her with that excuse. The poor girl, she was a wreck worrying about them."

Wiping a tear from her eye, Rosa continued, saying, "Peronne and his inner circle tend to do bad things to young women when they get the chance. She was different, though. Peronne had his eyes for her, more so than the others. After he had stalled her about the children as long as he could, he had several of the men bring her to his home."

"I wouldn't call it *his* home," Jack interrupted with contempt in his voice. "We all know how he came to live there."

"Anyway," she said, returning to the story, "This one was different. She was strong. She had seen and done a lot during her time out there traveling. I could see it in her eyes. I could see it in the way she resisted them. Not with rage, but almost as if she was manipulating them while they were attempting to manipulate her. Once they got her to Peronne's home, or rather, the home he calls his own, the game changed. She didn't give in to his attempts to woo her, and it hurt his ego. He's a very small man inside, if you ask me. That makes him dangerous. He has to compensate with violence and intimidation to cover his insecurities.

"To make a long story short, he drugged her to get what he wanted. She awoke in a very unflattering position. I knew the men had been taking advantage of her in very ugly ways while she was asleep. It sickened me. I had seen it before, but this one, for some reason, pushed me over the edge inside.

"Then one day, when I was working at his home, she asked me for help. I almost walked out. I almost ignored her and did nothing. I'm thankful now, though, that I didn't. Maybe God will forgive me for everything that I looked away from, if I somehow helped this one," she said as she broke down in tears.

"It's okay," Jack said, holding her by the hand. "What did you do? How did you help?"

"I left her with a corkscrew," Rosa replied. "I didn't do anything else. I simply left her with it, and she used it to earn her freedom. The two officers guarding Peronne's home were somehow taken out by her. When the others realized what had happened, they came for me. They beat me over and over, asking me if I knew where she'd gone. I said nothing. I didn't know anything to tell them. The funny thing is, leaving her a corkscrew didn't seem like much, but somehow, I knew she could take care of the rest. It was in her eyes."

"Ahhhh!" Jack exclaimed as Jessie and T. R. cinched a belt tight around the make-shift leg brace they had cobbled together from materials found in the room.

"Sorry, Jack, but your buddies from outside who circled around the building are gonna be on us hot and heavy before we know it. We've got to get out of here."

"How? Our door has been closed," Jack asked while pointing out their dilemma.

"We'll have to find a new one," Jessie replied. "If we can get to the upper floors and near a window, maybe we can reach our guardian angel for a little cover fire while we get ourselves out of here."

Looking nervous, T. R. replied, "There's got to be an army surrounding this place by now."

"I didn't say it was gonna be easy," Jessie replied. "Do you have a better idea?"

Thinking for a moment, T. R. asked, "So, there's no way around the dozer?"

"Nope," Jessie replied sharply. "The floor above collapsed onto the opening. It's nothing but rubble."

"There's one option, if it's true," T. R. said.

"Option?" Jessie queried. "True?"

"There's supposed to be an old tunnel leading under the courthouse grounds that was built as part of the original structure. Remember, this was the town of the likes of Billy the Kid. When this old courthouse was built, such things were still heavy on the minds and memories of the people who lived here. After Billy the Kid's escape from the Lincoln jailhouse, people thought it prudent to build discreet ways to move prisoners about, one of which, was an underground tunnel. The tunnel was said to have been designed for occaisions where a prisoner or witnesses, who may be sworn to testify against such criminals, could be safely brought in and out without being led up the front steps of the courthouse, right out in the open."

"Why didn't you mention that before?" Jessie asked with tension in his voice.

"It wouldn't do us any good on the way in if we don't know where it comes out," T. R. replied. "We wouldn't have known where to start, and it's not like we could have just walked around in plain sight, looking for the other end of the tunnel."

"If that's what we're doing, I need to get a message to Angela to pull out and fall back. They'll eventually pinpoint her location. I can't have her just sitting there all this time, waiting for us to come out the front door."

"Angela?" T. R. queried.

"She's our guardian angel," Jessie quickly answered. Turning his attention back to the group, he said, "Okay, before we get too far ahead of ourselves, let's try to find this underground exit. If we can't find it, then she'll just see us exit out the front door after all. If we do find it, we'll get in touch with her and let her know to fall back."

Nodding in agreement, Jack winced in pain.

"He's not doing very well," Rosa said, wiping the sweat from his brow.

"Yeah, let's get a move on," Jessie replied. "T. R. and I will look for the tunnel, if it's here, while you stay with Jack.

"I don't need a babysitter," Jack said as he rested his Glock on his chest. "You guys keep her safe."

"You keep an eye on her, then," Jessie said, winking at Rosa.

~~~~

Working their way through the darkened basement hallway, lighting their way with their weapon-mounted lights, Jessie and T. R. double-checked the rooms they had previously cleared for any signs of access to an underground tunnel.

Reaching the end of the hallway, where the bulldozer now rested blade down, after having crashed into the basement, bringing the floor above them crashing down, Jessie looked at T. R. with disappointment and said, "Well, so much for that. Must have been just a myth."

Disappointed, T. R. said, "Sorry, man."

As Jessie began to speak, he felt a cold draft flow through the rubble. Looking around, he started to work his way through the debris.

"What?" T. R. asked.

"Don't you feel that?"

"Feel what?"

"That draft. It's coming from down here, not from above," Jessie said as he began to push some of the debris out of the way. Shining his light into the damaged basement foundation, Jessie said, "Well, I'll be damned."

"What?" T. R. asked, pushing in close to see.

"We were sitting right on top of the damn thing the whole time. That's why the dozer came down on us. It collapsed the
~~~~

roof of the tunnel that it was sitting on top of while it was just churning away up there all that time."

"It looks like they must have bricked over it at some point," T. R. added.

"Yeah, so whether it's still open on the other end or not remains to be seen," said Jessie as he scratched his chin and contemplated their next move.

Looking at the damaged structure, T. R. asked, "Do you think it's still safe."

"Safe?" Jessie replied with a chuckle. "That's a very subjective term at the moment. I say we give it a go."

~~~~

With Jack and Rosa caught up on the plan, and Jack's leg stabilized as best they could for their trek through the dark, cramped tunnel, Jack said, "Angela. We've got to tell Angela to fall back."

"I'll do it," T. R. said. "Let me have the radio, I'll work my way up to the next floor where I can get out of this hole and get a signal. I'll catch up to you guys. Just get moving."

Handing T. R. his radio, Jack said, "Thanks, man. But you know the risk you're taking going up there alone, right? Who knows how many of Peronne's men are in the building by now."

"I know," T. R. replied. "I let you down big time when I didn't quit working for that son-of-a-b— as soon as I found out what he was really about. I'm not gonna let you or Angela down again."

With a smile, Jack put the radio down and took T. R.'s hand, shaking it, while looking him in the eye, saying, "It's not how you played the game in the past that matters. It's how you play it today that counts. You're still a true friend in my book. I'm sorry I treated you differently."
~~~~

"I'll always be the one who's sorry," said T. R. as he shook Jack's hand. "Now get going. I'll see you on the other side."

Staring at him with a confused expression, Jack started to say something as T. R. corrected himself, saying, "Other side of the tunnel."

"Oh, yeah, right," Jack said with a laugh.

## Chapter Twenty-Four

As a police SUV pulled up in front of the house, Leina watched from the second-floor window of the home where she cared for the woman who had taken her in to protect her. Still unconscious from the severe beating she took from Peronne's men, Leina's anger and rage grew inside as she dressed the woman's wounds as best she could.

Walking up to the other vehicle on scene, one of the officers asked, "Hey, what's the status?"

The officer that had remained inside the vehicle said, "Wilks and McCarthy went inside a while ago. They must be having fun because I figured they'd be out by now. I told them not to be too rough on the old lady. That sort of thing looks bad."

As the man on foot chuckled in reply, he said, "Maybe that cute little teenaged granddaughter of hers is in there. That might be what's taking them so long."

As he began to smile at the thought of his own statement, the top of his head exploded as a large section of his skull was torn away from the impact of a high-powered rifle bullet, splattering blood and brain matter on the light-colored desert tan vehicle behind him. His now lifeless body dropped to the ground with a sickening thud.

"S—!" the officer in the vehicle yelled as he floored the SUV and sped away, getting some distance between himself and the home.

Yelling out of the second-floor bedroom window, Leina shouted at the top of her lungs, "Stand up and fight, you cowards!"

Leaning the old .30-06 hunting rifle, which she had retrieved from the hidden compartment in the downstairs bathroom against the wall, Leina quickly slid the bed far away from the window to shield the unconscious woman from any potential returned fire.

Lifting her off the bed, Leina placed her in the corner of the room and covered her with a mattress to protect her from the flying debris that she felt was inevitable at this point. Mumbling under her breath, Leina said, “Come on, damn it. Let’s get this over with.”

Hearing the woman begin to moan, Leina hurried over to her, pulled the mattress slightly out of the way, and said, “Ma’am, are you okay?”

Watching her lips try to make words but hearing no sound, Leina leaned down closer and asked softly, “What? What can I do for you?”

“T… Tommy. They killed my Tommy,” she said, weak and barely able to remain conscious. “He was my youngest son. He was my last living child,” she said as tears began to roll down her cheeks.

Taking her by the hand, Leina said, “I’m so sorry. Those men will never hurt anyone again. None of their kind will, if I can help it.”

Coughing, and clearly in pain, the woman tried to sit up as Leina gently urged her to remain on the floor. “I’m sorry it’s not very comfortable, but it’s not over yet. I need you to stay here where it’s safe. I promise, I’ll take good care of you, as you did for me.”

Grasping Leina’s hand, the woman laid her head back on the pillow Leina had arranged for her on the floor and slipped back out of consciousness. With her grip loosening, Leina gently folded her arm across her chest and pulled the mattress back over her for protection.

Moving over to the window, Leina drew her Glock from its holster, checked that a round was in the chamber, removed the magazine, and checked the capacity. “Sixteen rounds in the mag and one in the pipe for seventeen," she said aloud as she laid the pistol to the side.

Next, she removed the other two magazines from the magazine pouch, noting that they were loaded to capacity as well. "49 rounds of nine millimeter," she said as she re-holstered the weapon and snapped the magazine pouch back onto her forcefully procured duty belt.

Picking up the plastic ammunition container she had taken from the underfloor compartment with the rifle, she flipped the latch on the side, swinging the lid open to find a mix of brands and projectile types of .30-06 cartridges. "There's got to be at least two hundred rounds here. That's a start."

Laying the rifle across her lap as she scooted her chair back away from the window, but still close enough to retain her view of the street below, Leina said, "Your move, boys."

## Chapter Twenty-Five

Watching T. R. disappear into the darkness of the basement hallway, Jessie turned to Rosa and Jack, saying, "Okay, let's get a move on. Jack, hand me that pack."

Removing the sling-style multi-cam pack from over his shoulder, Jack handed it to Jessie, saying, "Here ya go. But what are you gonna do with that?"

Inspecting it for quality of construction and strength, Jessie tugged on it, saying, "This thing is pretty sturdy."

"I never did buy cheap crap if it was something I wanted to be able to depend on. Those crappy but cheap Chinese-made packs you could get for twenty-nine dollars back in the day would have fallen apart by now."

"That thinking is paying off big time today," Jessie replied. Turning to Rosa, he said, "Here," handing it to her. "With Jack and I back to back, wrap this around us both, then buckle it together."

"What?" Jack queried.

"This tunnel is too cramped, especially with the collapsed ceiling in this first section, for you to hobble upright. With your busted up leg, you won't be able to crawl very well. I'll hunch over and crawl, dragging you along behind."

"To hell with that!" Jack exclaimed as if he had been insulted. "I can make it just fine."

"Come on, man. You know as well as I do that crawling with a broken leg stuck out straight in a splint will not be a picnic. Now, just suck it up and you can cover us from the rear as I go," Jessie said with a grin as he began to chuckle.

"What?" Jack again asked.

"You can be my tail-gunner."

With a perturbed look on his face, Jack replied, "I knew I should have shot you when I saw you creeping around my home."

Interrupting in a commanding voice, Rosa said, "Okay you two, no one's manhood is in question here. Let's just do what Jessie suggested and get going."

With a defeated tone in his voice, Jack's eyes responded in kind as he said, "Yes, ma'am," reluctantly putting his back up against Jessie's.

Tugging firmly on the strap, ensuring the fit was secure, Rosa said, "Okay, that's as good as it's gonna get."

Leaning forward and squatting, Jessie said, "I'm sure as hell glad you're a skinny fellow."

"There's not a lot of fat people left, these days. Except for rat bastards like Peronne, of course."

"Yeah, he's like the Kim Jong Un of Fort Sumner," Jessie said as he started to work his way through the rubble, hunching down close to the ground.

"Damn, man. I wish I would have known you when times were good. You must have been a hoot."

"Trust me. Be glad you're meeting me now, not long ago. You would have hated me. I didn't deal with things very well for quite some time."

"We've all been there, my friend. Trust me. We've all been there," Jack said as Jessie carried him over and through the rubble and into the old, long-abandoned tunnel.

~~~~

Working his way up the dark stairwell from the basement, T. R. paused to listen for any activity above. Hearing nothing but silence, he attempted to focus his eyes in the darkness, but to no avail. Avoiding the urge to flip on his weapon-mounted light, he
~~~~

ascended the stairs by feel, with his left hand on the railing while holding the pistol grip of his M4-style AR-15 carbine in his right.

Reaching the top of the staircase, T. R. felt around on the door to find a horizontal, bar-type push lever that spanned the width of the door on both sides. Pushing it slowly, the door began to open, exposing the light shining through the windows at each end of the hallway of the first floor.

Clearing the area as best he could from the stairwell, T. R. slowly worked his way into the hall, slicing the pie around the wall as he went. Standing in the hallway, being exposed from both sides, T. R. quickly moved toward the end of the building where Angela had been providing them with over-watch protection.

Attempting to turn the door handle to the room at the end of the hallway on the right, he thought, *Crap,* as he found it to be locked. Immediately moving to the other side of the hall, T. R. found the opposing door to be unlocked, quickly moving into the room, closing the door behind him.

With light shining through the half-drawn window shades of the long-abandoned administrative office, dust particles danced about, illuminated by the rays of light. Quickly moving over to the windows on the east-facing end of the building, T. R. looked around outside and was surprised not to see the might of Peronne's forces surrounding the building.

"Where the hell are they?" he thought aloud as he scanned the area, looking for external threats. "I was confident they would have shown up in force by now."

Picking up the radio, clicking it on, he pressed the transmit key and simply said, "Hey, Guardian Angel."

Releasing the transmit key, he listened for a response but heard nothing. Making a second attempt, he said, "Guardian Angel, are you still there?"

Pausing once again to listen, he heard, “Where’s Dad? Is he okay? Who is this?”

Pleased to hear Angela’s voice over the radio, knowing that she was indeed safe and sound, he replied, “He’s fine. It’s me, T. R. He’s hurt, but will be okay. He wanted me to tell you that we are taking an alternate route, and for you to fall back to Bravo Two.”

“What? Uh... okay,” she replied reluctantly, confused by what T. R. had said.

“By the way, what do you see around us? How many threats?” he asked.

“It’s pretty quiet. Two officers circled around the building, and I lost sight of them, but no more units have arrived.”

“That doesn’t make any sense at all,” T. R. replied. “Well, I’d better get...”

Interrupted by a solid thud to his back, followed by the sonic crack of a high-velocity muzzle report, T. R. fell forward into a desk and chairs, dropping the radio to the ground. Gasping for air as he rolled over to his back, he could barely breathe, feeling as if his lungs had been stolen from him. As panic began to set in, T. R. saw one of Peronne’s men standing in the doorway of the room, holding his patrol rifle.

“Die, you f—— traitor!” the man said as he raised his rifle for a second shot, aiming directly at T. R.’s head.

“No!” a second voice shouted from the hallway as Officer Lynch entered the room. “You don’t get to have all of the fun. I’ve been wanting to kill this little b— for a long damn time. Heck, I wanted to gut him even before he left his post. He was always the weak one. I knew he would crack.”

Keeping his rifle pointed squarely at T. R., the first man said, “Sure thing, man. Have fun,” as he motioned with his head toward T. R.

"I'm gonna take care of this the old-fashioned way," Lynch said with a smile on his face as he drew his knife from his belt. "Don't worry. You won't feel the burn for long. Actually, on second thought, maybe you will. I don't want the fun to be over too soon."

T. R. struggled to speak, but began to feel blood pooling in his lungs. He felt as if he was drowning in his own blood as the small amount of breathing capacity he had left began to be lost to the gurgling of blood in his chest.

As Lynch stood over him with a smile on his face, he held his knife in the light of the window, reflecting it off the shiny blade into T. R.'s eyes as if to taunt him one last time. As he started to kneel, exposing himself to the light, the window above T. R. shattered as Lynch was knocked several feet backward, blood exploding from his back as a bullet from Angela's rifle ripped directly through his heart.

Raising his rifle toward the window to counter the threat that Angela posed, the other officer took his eyes off T. R. for a split second, allowing T. R. to draw his sidearm, firing two shots directly into the man's chest, dropping him to the floor, dead on impact.

Being too weak to hold his pistol any longer, T. R. dropped his hand to the floor as he heard Angela's voice over the radio, "T. R.! Are you hit? Are you hit?"

Unable to speak in reply, he clicked the transmit key twice to acknowledge her in the affirmative.

Hearing her distressed voice once again, she asked, "Do you need help? What can I do?"

Clicking the transmit key once for no, T. R. knew there was nothing she could do to help him. He fully understood that he was down to his final few minutes on Earth, and there was no reason for her to expose her position or risk herself any longer.

Hearing her sobbing voice over the radio, she said, “I’m sorry. I wish I could have gotten a shot off sooner, but I didn’t know what room you were in until I saw the officer’s muzzle flash. I’m so sorry. I’ll tell Daddy you did it. I’ll tell him you went down fighting like a hero,” she said as her sobs overtook her voice.

Holding the radio to his chest, T. R. felt his world fade as he used his last ounce of strength to pull the radio to his face, transmitting his final word through his gurgling chest cavity wound, “G...Go...”

Hearing nothing but silence after that final transition, she waited a moment and asked, “Are you still there?” but heard nothing. No mic clicks, no sounds of any kind. With tears in her eyes, Angela picked up her rifle and prepared herself to fall back to her father’s pre-planned position as T. R. had relayed.

Transmitting one final time, her soft and gentle voice came over T. R.’s radio, saying, “Godspeed, my friend. Godspeed.”

## Chapter Twenty-Six

Reaching the end of the tunnel and what appeared to be a dead end, Jessie felt around in the darkness, looking for a way out. "Here," he said as he began to sit down, "Rosa, help Jack keep his leg stable while I sit. Then, you can undo the pack and cut us loose."

Doing as he asked, Rosa helped Jack to the ground as he grunted in pain.

"The throbbing is getting worse," Jack said with concern in his voice. It's a weird feeling...like something's not quite right. Even for a broken leg."

"Is there someone in town that can take a good look at it when this is all over?" Jessie asked.

"When it's all over? You're an optimistic fellow, aren't you," Jack said in reply to Jessie's comment.

"It'll all be over at some point," Jessie replied. "Whether you're around to get your leg checked out is what remains in question."

"Ha, ha, funny man," Jack replied.

Flipping on his light, Jessie scanned the area, looking for a way out. "I sure as hell hope we didn't crawl through all of this rat-poop infested muck for nothing."

Hearing the muffled sounds of gunfire echoing through the tunnel from the courthouse, Jessie's thoughts were interrupted by his fears of what T. R. might be facing.

"I wonder if he was the one doing the shooting?" Jack wondered aloud.

"That's impossible to say," Jessie replied. "I'll go back for him once we've got you two to safety."

"You're something else, you know that?" Jack said. "I mean, I just can't figure you out. You lost everything. En route to find your sister, you take a diversion to investigate something you found along the way, to help total strangers, and you keep risking your neck over and over again for something that I can't even figure out. What do you have to gain from it all? Are you trying to get yourself killed? I mean, you didn't know T. R. from Adam, you didn't know me, you didn't know Rosa, and you sure as hell don't know the woman or the kids. You could have just kept on going in safety and you wouldn't even know all of this was going on. But here you are. Do you have a death wish? Is this a suicide by another's hand kind of thing?"

Thinking for a moment before replying, Jessie said, "What point would there be in living if I had just kept going? If I kept avoiding trouble as I went, sure, I could stay alive for quite some time. I might even avoid danger long enough to live to be an old man, somewhere hidden from the world. But you know what? I was hidden from the world, and it found me anyway. No, I don't have a death wish, but I don't have a desire to wander this world like a coward or a ghost, either. If my life has no meaning, well, then it just..."

"I understand," interrupted Jack. "I understand completely."

Turning his attentions back to the task at hand, Jessie began searching the ceiling for a way out and noticed something of interest. Focusing his light on what appeared to be an old, rusty handle caked in layers of dirt and decay, he stood up in the cramped space the best he could, held the handle, and slammed his shoulder into the ceiling in an attempt to loosen the exit, if that was what he had found.

As several inches of dirt and dust fell from the ceiling of the filthy tunnel from the impact of his shoulder, Jessie, Jack, and Rosa all began to cough and fan the dirt-particle-filled air from their faces.

"Sorry about that," Jessie said, shining his light back to the ceiling. "I think I see the edges of the opening.

Placing his shoulder against it once again while holding on to the handle tightly, Jessie pushed with his legs as hard as he could, getting the large, heavy stone door to begin to move as he stood.

With light shining down into the tunnel, Rosa said aloud, "Thank you, God," as she clutched and kissed the Catholic rosary that hung around her neck.

Climbing up out of the tunnel and into the light, Jessie looked down and said, "Brilliant."

"What?" asked Jack, curious as to what they had found.

"We are in the graveyard across the street from the courthouse. We're literally crawling up out of a false grave inside of a granite family burial vault."

Chuckling through the pain, Jack said, "At least we're going in the right direction." Seeing that both Jessie and Rosa were confused by his statement, Jack clarified, "You know, coming out of a grave instead of going into one."

With a smirk, Jessie replied, "The day's not over yet."

"That's not funny," Rosa replied.

"Oh, I meant him," Jessie added. "I'm sure you and I will be all right, but him, well, who knows."

Changing the subject, Rosa said, "Let's get out of here. The thought of being beneath the graves isn't serving my nerves well."

"Yes, ma'am," Jessie replied as he forcefully slid the large, heavy stone door, that they now knew to be the lid to a tomb, inside of a false mausoleum.

Pulling himself up and out, Jessie squinted as the day's failing light shined through the mausoleum's stone window openings. Looking back down to Rosa and Jack, he said, "The sun will be gone soon. This mausoleum will be a good place to hide out until then. We can try to make a move under the cover of darkness.

Looking down to Jack, Jessie asked, "So, how do you want us to do this? You're the one that's gonna have to go through the hurt of it all."

"Just get me out of here. I can deal with it."

"Rosa," Jessie said while extending his hand. "You come on out. I'll go back down and lift Jack out while you pull from up here."

Taking his hand, Rosa climbed out of the tunnel and into the mausoleum. Once clear, she immediately took her rosary into her hand and said a prayer of thanks for being delivered from her captivity. Turning to Jessie, she tucked her rosary back into her shirt and said, "Okay, let's get him out."

Climbing back down into the tunnel, Jessie said, "If you sit on my shoulder, I can stand and lift you toward the opening. Swinging your busted leg over that stone edge at the top will be the tricky part. Keeping it good and straight, that is."

As Jack and Jessie positioned themselves to lift Jack out of the tunnel, Jessie added, "Oh, and one more thing."

"What's that?" asked Jack.

"If it hurts, try not to scream or make any noises. Remember, we're right across the street."

With a nod in the affirmative, indicating that he was ready and understood, Jessie stood, lifting Jack up and into the false tomb, where Rosa took his hands and began to pull him up and into the mausoleum. Reaching the edge of the tomb, Jack placed his hands on the stone while Rosa reached in and took hold of his leg, attempting to help Jack to swing it over the ledge.

Gritting his teeth through the pain as he had to bend his leg slightly to clear the structure, Rosa could see that Jack's pain was severe. Beads of sweat began to appear on his forehead, and his skin grew pale.

"Are you okay?" she asked.

Nodding in reply while breathing heavily, Jack's leg cleared the opening while Rosa helped him down to the floor where he could lie down and recover from the pain for a moment.

"Okay, we've got him," Rosa quietly said to Jessie down below.

Handing Jack's rifle up to Rosa, Jessie said, "Here. You two stay put. I've got to go back for T. R. He should have caught up with us by now. And those shots..."

"Be careful," she said with fear in her eyes. "Please don't leave us here alone. He's going to need medical attention very soon, and I can't get him there alone with Peronne's men out there."

"I'll be back. I promise," Jessie said in a reassuring voice.

~~~~

Slipping out of sight and back into the darkness of the tunnel below, Jessie worked his way back toward the courthouse, occasionally pausing to listen for any sounds that T. R. could be heading his way.

Reaching the rubble where the dozer had entered the building, Jessie climbed through the debris and into the basement corridor and began working his way toward the stairwell, leading to the above ground floors. Slipping into the stairwell, working his way up and around the stairs to the main floor above, Jessie paused and listened for activity.

Hearing nothing but silence, Jessie worked his way into the main floor hallway, uneasy about the silence. *This doesn't make sense. Where are Peronne's men? How did we assault one of their facilities without having them come down on top of us like a ton of bricks?*
~~~~

Clearing each room as he went, Jessie worked his way toward a room on the left at the end of the hall. The door to the room stood open, with everything around him eerily silent. As he approached the room, the silence was broken by a static-filled, incoming radio transmission.

> *All units report to the intersection of 2nd and Mc Gee. The female suspect has been located. Standoff in progress. All units report to the intersection of 2nd and Mc Gee. Standoff in progress. Shots fired. Officers down.*

Gripping his rifle tightly, double-checking with his thumb that the safety selector was in the fire position, Jessie raised his barrel to the high ready as he worked his way toward the door. Expecting to hear a reply from the officer in the room, Jessie waited for the opportunity, knowing that the officer would be momentarily distracted by the radio communications.

Hearing no response, or no activity of any kind, Jessie sliced the pie with his rifle around the door, making entry into the room, ready to engage the threat as it presented itself. As the last rays of the sun's light faded from the building, Jessie saw two dead officers laying on the floor in front of him. He quickly saw that the radio transmission had been coming from the belt-mounted radio of one of the dead officers.

Continuing his scan, Jessie saw T. R., lying still and lifeless by the window, in a pool of blood. Rushing to his side, Jessie touched him, to feel that his skin was cold and lifeless. "Ah, man. I'm so sorry," Jessie said as he closed T. R.'s eyes. "I'm sorry you won't make it back to your family. I'm sorry I treated you the way that I did. You really have redeemed yourself. You died a hero to us, serving others instead of yourself."

Hearing another radio transmission, this time, a very faint incoming transmission from the hand-held radio that T. R. had taken from Jack to reach Angela, Jessie heard:

*Are you still there? Are you okay? Please answer...*

Picking up the radio, Jessie pressed the transmit button and replied, "Angela?"

After a brief pause, he heard a woman's voice answer, "Yes."

"It's me, Jessie," he replied. "T. R. didn't make it." Looking up at the broken window and the way the glass was dispersed on the floor, Jessie said, "It looks like you were still his guardian angel, though."

"I tried," she replied through her tears.

"Are you safe?" he asked.

"Yes. I'm fine. How's Dad?"

"He busted up his leg, but he'll be okay. You just get somewhere safe, but not too far. Stay within radio range of the courthouse. I can't say where we'll be, but we'll be safe. Just keep yourself that way as well."

"Okay," she replied. "Tell Dad I love him."

"I will," Jessie said as he clipped the radio to his belt.

~~~~

With the day having fully given way to the night, Rosa peered anxiously out of the stone mausoleum's window as she watched for movement at the courthouse across the street.

"Don't worry," Jack said from behind her, laying on the floor with his leg elevated. "If Jessie ran into trouble, you'd have heard it by now."

After a few more minutes of silence, Rosa and Jack heard rustling from the tunnel below. Picking up his rifle, Jack
~~~~

prepared for the worst as they heard a faint voice say, "It's me, Jessie. I'm alone."

Climbing up into the mausoleum, Jessie dusted himself off and said, "T. R. didn't make it," as Rosa's eyes filled with tears.

"What happened?" Jack asked.

"Two of Peronne's men cornered him in one of the rooms. He did his job, though. He had made contact with Angela, and she's fine. It looked like she had even managed to provide him with a little bit of fire support during his struggle." Reaching to his belt, Jessie unclipped the radio and handed it to Jack, saying, "Here. She told me she's safe. I told her to stay within radio range of the courthouse, but to stay put for now. Oh, and she told me to tell you that she loves you."

Closing his eyes and silently saying, "Thank you, God," Jack turned to Jessie and said, "Now what?"

"The woman is held up near 2nd and Mc Gee. It sounds like she's holding her own for now."

"How do you know that?" Jack asked with a confused look.

"One of the dead officer's radios was still on. Peronne's men are all being called to the scene, which explains why they didn't rain hell down upon us. They've got other fish to fry. It sounds like she's taken a few of them out down there as well."

"Good girl," Jack said with a crooked smile.

Looking down at Jack's leg, Jessie asked, "How are you holding up?"

"It hurts like hell," Jack replied while rubbing his thigh. "It's throbbing like crazy, but all things considered, at least the bone isn't sticking out through the skin. A compound fracture would certainly have complicated things. I think I'll survive."

"Good, try and stay alive until morning." Looking to Rosa, Jessie said, "Keep an eye on him. Have him show you how to use that rifle of his. You never know what the night will bring."

With a concerned look on her face, Rosa looked to Jessie and asked, "Where are you going?"

"We've got to see this thing through. With Jack out of the fight..."

"I'm not out of the fight!" Jack interrupted.

"Okay, then," Jessie said, rewording his statement, "With Jack not in any condition to go sprinting from house to house, the best chance we have is to take advantage of Peronne's distraction with the woman. Not to mention the fact that she could use our help. I'll do my best to be a thorn in their side, distracting them from their task at hand. Where that will lead is anyone's guess at this point, but it's all we've got. We've already stirred the pot. Life isn't gonna go back to normal for you folks while Peronne is still in power, so we've got to try and fix that."

## Chapter Twenty-Seven

As the sun finally disappeared over the western horizon, darkness fell over the streets of Fort Sumner, and with it, the dreadful uncertainty of what might come. Leina knew that Peronne and his men would use the cover of darkness to make their move on her, but when? How? The only thing she knew for certain was that her odds of seeing another sunrise in this world were slim. That was okay with her, though. Her husband, her friends, and now her children, had all been taken from her. She felt as if she had nothing more to live for, and if she went down swinging, nothing would feel quite so fitting. Her only concern at this point was the woman who had risked and lost everything to take her in and offer her shelter in her time of need.

Looking over at the woman, hidden underneath the mattress, Leina reaffirmed her will to fight. There were still good people in this wretched, God-forsaken world and she would do her very best to protect this wonderful lady whom she didn't even know, until the very end.

The sound of a familiar voice rang over a public address system, interrupting her thoughts, saying, "Leina'ala. We offered you everything. We offered you safety. We offered you a future. And this is how you repay us? You murder our officers and take that poor woman hostage? You know we can't let this stand."

"You lying bastard!" she yelled toward the window in a fit of rage. "You murdered my friends. You took my children. You've taken everything from me, and all you offered me in return is servitude to you and your little kingdom! Well, I've got news for you, you dirty son-of-a-b—. I don't know how you've kept the good people of this town from taking up arms against you all this time, but your reign of terror ends now. I won't stand for it. I won't allow you to impose your will on these people or any more passersby out on the roads, even if it costs me my life doing so. Your crimes simply won't stand!"

Pausing for a moment, Chief Peronne answered in a very calm and collected voice, "Oh, it will cost you your life. I can promise you that."

~~~~

Climbing into one of the police SUVs left at the courthouse by Peronne's men, Jessie started the engine, switched on the lights, and said to himself aloud, "Why do I feel like I've been here before?"

Shifting the transmission into gear, Jessie began speeding down Sumner Avenue to the west. Approaching 2nd Street, Jessie hung a hard right and said to himself, "Mc Gee Avenue should be just up ahead."

Seeing several patrol SUVs in what appeared to be a defensive position around a small, two-story single-family home, Jessie saw an officer wave him over, seeming to give directions on where he was to position himself.

Slowing the vehicle, appearing to acquiesce to the officer's request, Jessie watched as the man seemed to be taking extra effort to look into the vehicle to identify the driver. "Here goes," he said as he shoved the accelerator to the floor, spinning the rear tires of the SUV wildly on the dry, dusty road.

Smashing the hood of his car into the officer, Jessie slammed on the breaks, throwing the man violently to the ground. He then brought his AR-10 to bear, firing as rapidly as he could through the window of the SUV, causing the other officers, who had previously been taking positions of cover from the potential fire from the house, to scatter like rats.

Throwing the transmission into reverse, Jessie backed away as fast as he could, reaching the engine's peak RPM, bouncing
~~~~

off of the rev-limiter as he fired the last round from his twenty-round 7.62 NATO magazine, locking the bolt firmly to the rear.

Smashing through a stop sign and the chain-link fence of one of the neighboring homes, Jessie felt the SUV slam to a stop as it crashed into the wooden steps leading up to the home's main entrance.

With Peronne's men beginning to regroup, Jessie swung the door open and ran out of the vehicle and behind the house, vanishing into the darkness of the night.

~~~~

Hearing the commotion and rapid-fire gunshots from across the street, Leina watched as a strange man in one of Peronne's SUVs seemed to be attacking his own men from their flank. As the vehicle sped away in reverse, firing wildly through its own windshield, Leina took advantage of the confusion. Taking aim on one of Peronne's men who was illuminated by the retreating vehicle's headlights, she placed the crosshairs of the scope on his chest, and slowly pulled the trigger until she felt the powerful .30-06 cartridge shove the rifle firmly into her shoulder, simultaneously dropping the man as the bullet tore clean through his torso.

Quickly cycling another round into the chamber with the bolt, Leina took aim once again as the men began to take cover behind their vehicles. She let another one-hundred-and-eighty grain, thirty-caliber projectile fly, striking one of the officers in the right shoulder, impacting the man so hard it spun him nearly all the way around before he fell to the ground.

Ducking back into the safety of the room as she saw a muzzle flash from the rifle of one of the men who had managed to take cover, Leina felt a high-speed 5.56 millimeter round whiz
~~~~

by her head as the officer managed to return fire with his AR-15 patrol rifle.

"Who the hell is that?" she shouted aloud, wondering who the mysterious man in the SUV was.

~~~~

Stopping several houses away to gather his bearings and regroup, Jessie pressed the magazine release button on his AR-10, dropping the empty magazine to the ground, quickly replacing it with a fresh OD green twenty-round polymer PMAG. Bumping the bolt catch release with the palm of his left hand, Jessie double-checked that a round was in the chamber and took refuge behind an old backyard shed that had become surrounded by tall weeds from neglect.

Hearing several gunshots being fired into the vehicle he had just abandoned, Jessie thought, "Idiots," as he patiently waited for them to round the corner of the home in pursuit.

After several moments, he heard the whispers of two of the men as they worked their way around the home. Seeing the light of their flashlights stop just short of rounding the corner of the house, Jessie readied his rifle, aiming it where he assumed they would appear next. *Come on, damn it. Don't make me wait on you all night,* he thought as he heard movement coming from the house behind him. *Crap!*

Overhearing a faint radio communication coming from the direction of the two men who had stopped short of Jessie's position, Jessie came to the realization that they would be boxing him in, closing in tight on his position. Being near the intersection of 3rd Street and Richards Street, Jessie knew that once his position was discovered, the men could easily call for backup, sending Peronne's men driving right up on him, leaving him with little way out.
~~~~

Slipping his sling around his shoulder, Jessie positioned his rifle across his back and crawled slowly and quietly to the edge of the fence behind the old shed. *Damn it. Chain-link,* he thought, realizing the easiest but most obvious way to get past the fence was to go over it.

Feeling around the bottom of the fence, Jessie could hear the men closing in on his position as they swept the surrounding houses in a very deliberate manner. *They're not gonna let this go. Their entire assault on the woman in the house is in jeopardy as long as I'm alive and on the loose, and they know it.*

Lifting up on the bottom of the fence, Jessie realized there was just enough room to slide underneath. Reaching around and pulling his rifle around in front of him, Jessie slid it underneath the fence and began to crawl as low to the ground as he could under the metal mesh and through to the other side.

With his head and his right arm and shoulder underneath, he felt a snag on his clothing, stopping his advance while he maneuvered, trying to free himself. *What, am I Peter Rabbit, now?*

As he calmly and quietly tried to free himself, a vehicle came around the corner from Richards Street, shining its headlights onto 3rd Street, and right in front of Jessie. Quickly retreating back into the yard, Jessie's shirt tore loose from the fence as the vehicle rounded the corner and began to work its way up 3rd.

*Damn it!* Jessie thought as his heart pounded in his chest, realizing that his rifle was still on the other side of the fence. Hearing a radio transmission from one of Peronne's men on foot getting closer and closer to his position, and with the vehicle's spotlight shining its way up the fence line, Jessie knew he had to abandon his beloved AR-10 and make his move before it was too late.

Quickly slipping across the home's weed-filled, abandoned lawn, Jessie made it to the side of the home as the vehicle's spotlight shone directly on his rifle as the vehicle came to a stop.

Making his move, Jessie ran around the corner of the house and ran straight into one of Peronne's men, knocking both of them to the ground. With Jessie lying on top of the man with the officer's AR-15 patrol rifle pinned between the two, he grabbed the officer's hand as he reached for his sidearm, shoving downward, keeping the pistol securely holstered while the two men struggled.

With his left hand on the man's gun, Jessie quickly grabbed the man's windpipe with his right and began to squeeze as hard as he could, stopping the man's call for help as he struggled to get his words past Jessie's crushing grip. Digging his fingers deeper and deeper into the man's throat, Jessie focused all of his rage on his task, resisting the man's attempts to get his fingers underneath Jessie's, in order to pry his hand free.

Feeling the man's windpipe collapse, the struggle began to fade as the man's eyes rolled back and his muscles relaxed, his life slipping away from him, taken from him with Jessie's bare hand.

Hearing the man's partner yell from the next yard over, "We found something," as he began to run toward Jessie's now illuminated rifle. Using this momentary distraction to his benefit, Jessie got off the slain officer, removed his rifle from its sling, unclipped his belt-mounted radio, and slipped off into the shadows of the night.

~~~~

Back in the elderly woman's home, Leina knew she had to stay on the move inside the home to prevent Peronne's men from carrying out an assault on her and the woman too easily.
~~~~

"The bathroom," she thought, remembering the hidden compartment beneath the floor where the woman had kept her safe.

Frantically dragging the mattress off the woman, Leina pulled her up and into a fireman's carry as she began to work her way through the house and down the stairs, carrying the rifle awkwardly with one hand while she held on to the woman with the other.

Reaching the downstairs bathroom, Leina nearly slipped and fell with the woman, slipping in the blood that had oozed underneath the door from the man she had disemboweled in such a gruesome fashion. Opening the door, Leina stepped over the man's body and laid her rifle on the bathroom sink so that she could properly take care of the woman. With her other hand now free, she opened the closet door, knelt down on her right knee, and pulled the hidden opening to the side.

Working her way into the compartment first, Leina carefully laid the woman inside, pushed her hair out of the way, and said in a soft and gentle whisper, "I'll come back for you. I promise. But if I don't, may God keep you safe and grant you the ability to get yourself out of here and to safety."

Climbing back up and out of the underfloor compartment, she reinstalled the false floor and scattered towels and other bathroom items around to mask the entrance.

As she reached for the old .30-06 hunting rifle, Leina was startled by the sound of a transmission coming through the dead officer's radio. Through gritted teeth, she heard an ominous, static filled transmission:

> *What's the matter, boys? Can't find me? How many of you have to die tonight before you realize you're following a dead man? That's right. Peronne, as well as all who follow him, will die tonight. You're all guilty of the worst of all*

*betrayals. You aren't just guilty of betraying your fellow man, you're guilty of betraying your entire community. You've killed for him. You've watched the innocent suffer. You've kept a tyrant and a madman in power, betraying every single person in this town. Your uniforms are supposed to represent service to the people with whom you share the town. Instead, you've turned your badge into a symbol of dishonor. You've betrayed your oath. You've betrayed your duty. You've betrayed everything that badge is supposed to represent. You don't serve the people. You serve a tyrant, and tonight, you will lie in the same pool of blood as him. Tonight, justice will finally be served upon you for all of the injustices you've perpetrated on your fellow man.*

As silence once again fell upon the radio, the thoughts of what may be going on began to swirl through Leina's mind. As she tried to piece it all together, she heard Peronne's familiar, angry voice scream through the radio:

*Who are you, you son-of-a-b—? You're the one that's gonna be lying in a pool of blood tonight, but you won't die right away. My men will kill you slowly. You'll feel the pain as I remove every finger from your hand, every toe from your feet, and every tooth from your mouth. I will disassemble your entire body until you die from the pain of it all. How dare you come into my town and threaten me. How dare you, you son-of-a-b—! You're gonna die, I tell you! Gonna die!*

Leina couldn't help but smile at how a man who liked to seem so in control, so calm, and so collected, was coming apart over the radio. *That psychotic coward is shaking in his boots,* she thought. *You can hear the trembling in his voice, disguised as rage.*

Hearing Peronne's angry voice once again, she heard him shout over the radio:

*Show yourself, you coward. Come out here and fight me like a man.*

*Is it manly to kill the innocent?* the strange man who had attacked Peronne and his men replied. *Is it manly to surround a house with overwhelming force to attack a woman? A woman, who you kidnapped, killing all of her friends and taking her children? Does that make you a man? All it makes you is a tyrant and a coward, and for that, you will pay and pay dearly. As for the rest of you, drop your weapons and walk away. It's your only chance.*

In an increasingly frustrated and angry tone, Peronne responded, *If you want to defend that woman, you'll die with that woman. I'll kill her in front of you, you son-of-a-b—! I'll give you a front row seat. I may even make you kill her yourself.*

*I think your men need an example to follow,* the voice said in a bone-chilling manner.

*The only example they need is to watch how I kill you with my bare hands!* Peronne shouted.

*Mustache...* the strange voice said, followed by the supersonic crack of a rifle as one of Peronne's officers in the perceived safety of their offensive position against the house violently fell forward onto the hood of his own SUV, as his forehead exploded from being shot squarely in the back of the head.

As Peronne's men began to scatter, Leina ran to the living room of the home and opened fire on them as they broke cover, realizing that the offending shot had come from directly behind them. Striking one of them in the side, dropping him to the ground, the man began flopping around like a wounded animal while screaming in agony. Leina cycled the bolt, chambering another round, this time aiming through the glass of one of the patrol vehicles. Taking the shot, her bullet struck a man squarely in the back as he tried to get a fix on the unknown shooter.

As return fire began shattering the ground-floor windows of the home, Leina dove to the floor, taking cover behind the old, leather sofa while she covered her head with her arms, shielding herself from the flying glass and debris that now filled the room.

As the gunfire subsided, Peronne's voice once again came over the radio in a fit of rage, now bordering on madness:

> *G— damn you, you son-of-a-b—! Tell me your name so that I can mark your grave when I bury what's left of you. I would feed you to the animals, but I need a gravestone with your name on it to piss on every day when I think about how much fun I had killing you!*

In a calm and collected voice, Leina heard the strange man reply:

> *I'm just a simple shepherd who lost everything I held dear because of the betrayal of men like you. And as a shepherd, one thing my life revolved around was killing any predators that threatened my flock. Killing you will be no*

*different. You're just a predator, preying on your fellow citizens. Nothing more, nothing less.*

Taking advantage of the lull in the fight while Peronne's men regrouped, Leina slipped out the back door of the home under the cover of darkness. Working her way around the block, she set out in an attempt to try to gather any intel she could on the current positions and the state of Peronne's men, considering the recent turn of events. She had no idea who the mysterious man wreaking havoc on Peronne and his men was, but she knew the chaos he was causing was an opportunity for her to inflict as much damage as she could, as well.

Noticing that Peronne had divided his men up into two distinct formations, one facing the home that she and the woman occupied, while the other covered their rear and flanking positions in an attempt to counter the strange man's harassing fire.

*They're not gonna be able to make an aggressive move on me so easily with their attention divided like this. All we need now is for dissension in his ranks to create even more chaos,* she thought as she looked back toward the home.

To her horror, Leina saw glowing orange flickers of light that appeared to be growing rapidly from within the first-floor living room of the house. She then saw a burning object being hurled into one of the shot-out front windows, intensifying the brightness almost immediately upon impact.

Her heart racing as thoughts of the woman in the hidden underfloor compartment flashed through her mind, Leina began to sprint back toward the home, no longer attempting to remain unseen by Peronne and his men. As gunfire erupted around her, she ran directly into the side door of the home, which was now engulfed in flames. The intense heat and overpowering fumes forced her to the floor, where she crawled in an attempt to reach the bathroom where she had left the woman beneath the floor.

Pulling her shirt up over her face, Leina tried her best not to inhale the noxious fumes as she began coughing uncontrollably. With only feet to go to reach the bathroom, Leina could see the growing flames flickering as a reflection in the drying pool of blood on the floor, blood that had been flowing out beneath the bathroom door.

Feeling her strength begin to fade, Leina started to lose all control as her coughing intensified and her eyes burned from the smoke and fumes. Screaming, “Noooooo!” as the fire grew around her, Leina’s world faded to darkness as the smoke and fumes overtook her.

## Chapter Twenty-Eight

Coughing herself awake, Leina awoke in a panic, her last memory being that of the light of flames from within the bathroom she had so desperately tried to reach in time. Frantically looking around the room, she heard the familiar voice of the man on the radio, who said, "Shhhh. It's okay. You're safe. Peronne doesn't know where we are at the moment, though they are searching house to house, so it may only be a matter of time."

Coughing and attempting to clear her throat to speak, he handed her a glass of water, saying, "Here, drink this. Your throat is probably quite irritated from the smoke."

Swallowing a drink of water, she struggled to speak, saying only, "Who...?

"My name is Jessie. Jessie Townsend," he stated in a calm and reassuring voice.

Speaking softly, she replied, "The radio... You're the man from the radio."

"Yes, ma'am."

As memories of the night began to flood back into her mind, her heart raced as she thought of the woman. "The woman!" she shouted. "Where is she?"

"Woman? What woman? You're the only person I could get to in the home. You were trying to get to the bathroom, which was fully engulfed in flames."

As tears began to roll down her cheeks, Leina sobbed and said, "She helped me. She was a total stranger and helped me when I was on the run. Peronne's men killed her son and beat her severely while trying to find me. She had hidden me in a secret underfloor compartment in that bathroom. That's where I had left her during the fighting. She was too weak and injured to get away, so I had resolved to stay with her until the end, helping her as she had helped me."

"I... I'm sorry," Jessie replied as he bowed his head for a moment to give her time to take it all in.

After a few moments, Leina asked, "Why? I mean, what brought you into my fight?"

Sitting on the bed next to her, he said, "This should be everyone's fight, not just yours. That's the problem. That's why men like Peronne are able to take control of an entire population of people who could and should be able to stand up and take their town back. Everyone is just afraid to be the first one killed, or they're afraid to be the only one in the crowd who stands up. It's easy to be a patriot when the battle lines are formed. It's not so easy to be the first to make the call to arms."

"Is this your town?" she asked, still confused.

"No, ma'am," he replied. "Before everything went down and the world quickly spiraled out of control, I was the sheriff of Montezuma County, Colorado. Before it got ugly, I moved onto a mountain homestead with my family to hide from it all. That worked for a while, and we had a great life, but eventually, the evil in the world will find you. You can't avoid it forever. Choosing to sit something out simply doesn't work, at least not in the long run."

Bending and unwinding a paperclip he had found lying on the floor in a nervous fashion, Jessie tossed it aside, and continued, "To make a long and painful story short, my family was killed, and everything I held dear in this world was taken from me, even my horse. After I had set out on a mission to find my sister, whom I haven't seen or heard from since long before this all started, I swore to never sit something out again. As I traveled east, just north of here, I heard a barrage of gunfire one evening as I made camp a safe distance from town. The next morning, I investigated and found what appeared to be an ambush site. There were signs of children, so I simply couldn't keep going without looking into it further."

Pausing, noticing that his observations were bringing Leina's memories back to the forefront of her mind, he said, "So, anyway, once I started surveillance of the town, I encountered one of Peronne's men who had slipped away in the middle of the night to escape the goings on in Fort Sumner. He wanted nothing to do with it, yet after speaking to him long and hard about it, he realized that he couldn't just run away, either. He knew it would eat at him for the rest of his life if he didn't try to right his wrongs."

In an attempt to break her trance-like state, he asked, "Were you held by Peronne and his men at his home?" he asked.

Pausing for a moment before replying, Leina said, "Yes. Yes, I was. How did you know?"

"Did you encounter a woman of Hispanic descent, named Rosa?"

"Uh... yes, yes I did. How did you know that?" Leina asked inquisitively.

"The man who fled Peronne knew quite a bit of the goings-on in town, and he knew some people who he thought might have been able to help. Help they did, which led us to Rosa."

"Is she okay?" Leina asked, worried that the woman's involvement in her escape may have led to something horrible for her.

"She's okay now," Jessie replied. "T. R., he's the man who fled and then teamed up with me, died as we made a move on one of Peronne's assets where they kept her." Looking to the floor to gather his thoughts, Jessie solemnly said, "I guess you could say he made good on vindicating himself. Anyway, she was safe when I left her to come here. She told us everything she knew about your situation, and putting two plus two together, I assumed you were a victim of the ambush."

Nodding in the affirmative, Leina wiped a tear from her eye and said, “Yes, that was us. They killed all of the other adults, but took the children and me. I haven’t seen them since I got here. Peronne kept promising to return them to me, but it was all a ruse to get me to...” Pausing to search for the words, Leina changed the course of the conversation, saying, “So, where are the others? The others that helped you rescue Rosa. Are they out here with us somewhere, also?”

“One of them was injured pretty bad. Rosa is caring for him now. The man’s daughter helped us also. She’s safe as far as I know, but I haven’t had reliable enough contact to know her exact whereabouts or intentions. For all practical purposes, we have to assume it’s just you and me for now.”

“That suits me just fine,” Leina replied. “I’ve resigned myself to the fact that I will die killing him if need be, and I’m at peace with that.”

“Neither of us will die if I can help it, but I agree with you. A life not lived to the fullest is a life not worth living, and that doesn’t just go for the pleasures in life. That’s another one of the things that led the world down the path it was on. Everyone was so consumed by their own personal gain, happiness, and comfort, that none of us stood together to do the hard things. The wicked and the corrupt took full advantage of our brain-dead, reality-TV-consumed, self-centered society and pushed our once-polite society to the breaking point and beyond. Sadly, they did it before our very eyes, yet no one hardly even noticed.”

“My husband, Cas, used to say the same things,” she said, smiling at the warm memories she still held of her late husband.

“Where is he? If I may ask,” Jessie asked carefully.

“Let’s just say you and I have similar pasts,” Leina replied as she looked around the room. Changing the subject once again, she said, “So, what’s the plan?”

"I've had a pretty simple plan so far," Jessie replied, "but the usefulness of that plan is about to end. The sun is almost up, and it's going to make being a ghost that pokes at Peronne's men until his ranks start to crumble a little harder. There's no way to take on their numbers head on, but if we can chip away at his men's morale, and cause them to question their allegiance to such a tyrant and a monster, then we might have a chance. As long as we can stay alive in the process, that is."

"We're gonna need a better plan than that," she said. "Unless, of course, we can lie low until tonight."

"I doubt that would work very well," Jessie replied. "With the cover of darkness gone, Peronne will be emboldened to tear this town apart until they find us. No one has ever hit him so hard or embarrassed him so much. He's not gonna let this stand. He's not gonna just let it wash away. No, he's gonna need to make a point, and strong point, with us, to keep the rest of the people in town at bay. A tyrant who feels that he has had a chink in his armor revealed will be quick to make a show of force, and more than likely, he will do it in a very brutal way."

Interrupted by an incoming radio transmission, both Jessie and Leina stopped to listen, hearing:

> *Hello, there, shepherd. You may think you've put yourself in a position of power, but you're wrong. All you've done is endanger your flock. I'm going to start preying on your sheep if you don't show yourself soon. Baaaaaa baaaaa baaa...*

"What? What's he gonna do?" she asked.

"I imagine he's threatening to do people harm in an attempt to lure me out. That's not a wise move. If he inflicts acts of brutality against the innocent, the population he's trying to control, he could lose his most important aspect of control—

their willingness to continue to sit on the sidelines to preserve their own safety. His desperation is setting in quicker than I thought," Jessie replied. "That's not good. Things are gonna get real ugly, really fast."

"Are you going to reply?" she asked.

"No, I'm done with the radio for now. They've had time to gather themselves together and get their hands on radio direction finding gear that I would imagine a department such as theirs would have been before the collapse would have on hand. He's probably taunting me to reply so that they can DF our position and move in. No, we'll hold off on using the radio again."

"What do you have for weapons?" she asked. "I had a rifle, but it was lost in the home. All I have is this..." reaching for her sidearm, she realized it was no longer there.

"Relax," Jessie said reassuringly. "Your Glock is right here. I merely removed it because I wasn't sure what state you would be in when you awoke. I didn't want you to think I was one of them and get myself shot."

Reaching the duty belt with the holstered Glock to her, he added, "I've got an AR-15 I picked up from one of Peronne's men. I lost my personal rifle in the insanity of the night as well. Other than that, all I have is my old Colt, here," he said, patting his open hand on the side of his old leather cowboy-style holster. "Oh, and a compound bow and several broadhead arrows I found in one of the closets upstairs. You never know when something like that will come in handy," he said, pointing to the bow he had securely tied to a small pack he had found as well.

"We're gonna need to do better than that," she replied. "Two pistols and a rifle aren't gonna get us far against these guys."

"They'll get us far enough," he replied with confidence. "Now, you get some rest while I stand watch. You've had a rough night, and I can't imagine today being anything other than a rough day. Let's take advantage of the remaining darkness to sit and rest for a while, because with the rising sun, trouble will come."

## Chapter Twenty-Nine

With his boots propped up on the nightstand next to the bed where Leina slept, reclining in an office chair he found in the study of the abandoned home, Jessie's eyes felt heavy as he gazed out the window on the other side of the room. Jessie was thankful for the illumination the full moon was providing them, helping him to keep an eye on the goings-on in the surrounding neighborhood.

Chills ran up Jessie's spine as he heard a low and ominous growl coming from just outside the window. Standing up slowly, drawing his trusty old Colt from its holster as he crept across the room, Jessie's heart skipped a beat to see a large, gray wolf standing just outside the window, its fangs exposed with the blood of a fresh kill still dripping from its muzzle.

As the wolf raised its head toward the moonlit sky, it let out a spine-chilling howl as other wolves in the pack began howling all around the house.

Nearly falling out of his chair as he was startled awake, Jessie reached for his Colt, almost dropping it on the floor, still in a half-awakened state of confusion. Realizing it was only a dream, Jessie's spine tingled. *Something is wrong!* he thought as he shook Leina by the arm, awakening her from her much-needed rest.

"What, what is it?" she asked, trying to focus her eyes as she looked frantically around the room for a threat.

"We've got to get the hell out of here," Jessie said with a look of panic on his face.

"What? What is it?" she again asked.

"No time. Just come," he said as he grabbed his rifle and pack, peeking out the window. Seeing one of Peronne's SUVs parked just down the street, almost out of sight, he said, "Crap. Let's move."

Leading Leina down into the basement, Jessie hurried over to a window that was built into the block foundation of the home. Having previously stacked several boxes beneath the window, preparing it in advance for such an occasion, he said, "The moonlight is on the other side of the house. It should be dark along the foundation. I'll climb out and stay low. Once I determine it's safe, I'll help you out, and we'll make a run for that old metal garage behind the house across the street. We'll make a plan up on the fly from there, based on what we see."

Trusting Jessie's insistence in the matter, Leina watched as he climbed atop the boxes, tilted the window open, and pulled himself up and outside. After a quick scan of the area, she saw Jessie reach down into the basement from the outside, saying, "Come on."

Working her way outside and alongside the house as Jessie recommended, Leina whispered, "What is it?"

"I don't know, but trust me," he said again, insistently.

As he looked around trying to assess the situation further, Jessie and Leina were both startled by a loud and powerful impact of a battering ram smashing through both the front and back doors of the house simultaneously, followed by the concussive blast of what appeared to be flash-bang grenades.

"Now!" he said as the two began running across the lawn, hidden in the shadows of the moonlight toward the old, metal garage as planned.

Ducking behind the garage, in between the adjacent neighborhood street, a row of trashcans, and several overgrown shrubs, Leina grabbed Jessie by the arm and asked, "How the hell did you know they were coming?"

"I didn't," he replied, still scanning the area for more threats.

"What?" she asked, confused by his short and nonsensical answer.

"I'll explain later," he said, fixated on the SUV parked just fifty yards from their current position up the adjacent street.

"It looks like there is only one man by that vehicle. They must have had him standing watch on the perimeter while they made their move. I would assume each of the streets surrounding the house will have similar watches," Jessie said, explaining their situation.

"Are you sure he's alone?" she asked.

"It looks like it. I wouldn't normally expect them to leave a critical position staffed with only one man, but they do have fewer officers on the roster now than they did at the start of the day yesterday."

"I've gotten around seven of them, myself," she said. "I've lost track, though."

Glancing at her with an impressed look on his face, Jessie said, "Damn, that's... that's impressive and scary all at the same time. I'm glad I took your pistol until you awoke," he said with a chuckle.

"Don't mess with a momma bear's cubs," she replied.

"Good point," he said. "Okay, back to our friend out there by the SUV. If we can take him down, we can get our hands on a second rifle and some ammo that we will desperately need sooner rather than later."

"Just how do you plan on doing that without alerting the rest of them?"

Pulling the pack off his shoulder, Jessie removed the bow, took an arrow from its quiver, and secured the nock of the arrow at the nock loop.

"Are you sure you can hit him from here... in the dark?" she asked, uneasy about Jessie's intentions.

"With my own bow, yes. Not knowing exactly how the pins on this sight are sighted in, or if it's even sighted in at all... no. I can assume the yardage for each of the fiber-optic sight pins, and estimate the yardage to the target, and if it's set up the way I hope, I can pull it off. If not, well, we run, because he will be on the radio as soon as the arrow bounces off of whatever it hits."

As he drew the bowstring back to full-draw, Jessie said, "Damn, I wish I had a mechanical release. If you've got a better idea, now is the time to share it with me."

"Make it count," she replied.

"Roger that. Here goes," he said as he floated what he assumed was the fifty-yard pin on the target, controlled his breathing, and let the string fly, following through with his hold until the arrow had cleared the bow and was on its way to the target at over three-hundred feet per second.

With a deep thud, the arrow struck the man in the gut, just below his ballistic vest, dropping him instantly to his knees. Seeing him writhe around in pain, Leina sprang to her feet and sprinted toward him with everything she had as Jessie watched her pounce on top of the injured man with extreme violence of action, stabbing him repeatedly in the neck until he fell over, dead upon impact with the ground.

Running up to her side, Jessie saw her breathing heavily with blood splatter on her face. He stood there for a brief moment, speechless to what he had just witnessed.

Looking at him while wiping the blood from her face with her own shirt, she said in a calm and collected voice, "He was gonna die, but wasn't dead. He had a radio and a gun. He could have given it all away."

"Good job," Jessie replied, still in awe of her actions. Releasing his duty belt to retrieve his radio and sidearm, Jessie shoved it into his pack while Leina unclipped the sling of man's rifle, removing it from around his body.

Searching the SUV for anything else of use, Jessie heard over the vehicle-mounted radio:

*The house is clear. They were here, but are gone.*

Followed by a profanity-laced tirade in Peronne's voice:

*G— damn it! Get that son-of-a-b— and that wh—! Tear this town apart until you find them! Kill anyone who gets in your way! I want them, and I want them now!*

Removing a pen and a notepad from the vehicle, Jessie wrote a note and tacked it to the man by shoving the pen into his flesh. Leina looked at the note, which read, *If you keep serving Peronne, we will keep stalking you.*

Looking at Leina, Jessie said, "Never miss an opportunity to f— with the enemy's mind. Get in his head and stay there. Never relent."

Nodding in agreement, the two slipped away into the darkness just as an SUV from the raid on the house reached the scene. Turning to watch for just a second, Jessie and Leina saw the men reading the note. Wasting no further time, they slipped away from the scene, putting as much space between them and the officers as they could.

## Chapter Thirty

Slowly working their way across town under the cover of the remaining darkness, Jessie and Leina could see the sun shining its first rays of morning light over the eastern horizon. "Our cover is almost blown," Jessie said, admiring the beauty of the glowing orange horizon. "You know, I've always had a thing for sunsets and sunrises. We had magnificent views from our Rocky Mountain homestead. Sunrise was when I would have my first cup of coffee in the morning, and sunset was when I would have my first sip of wine at night. Although I no longer have that life to celebrate with the rising and setting of the sun, I still hold onto them as my most favorite moments of the day. These days, the sunrise lets me know I have at least one more day on Earth to leave my mark, and the sunset lets me know I survived another day."

"Pretty deep thoughts for a man who doesn't hesitate to kill," Leina said, remarking about the complexity of Jessie's personality.

"I don't hesitate when, in my opinion, the person on the other end of my gun, my knife, or in last night's case, my bow, has voluntarily put themselves in a position where their death is required so that others can live. Peronne's men, for example, choose to kill and oppress others. So the way I see it, they are the ones making the decision to die, more so than I am making the decision to take their life. The lives of the innocent and the good are what matter in this world, not the lives of the wicked. The wicked have a choice. They don't have to go down that path."

"Have you ever killed someone who wasn't...wicked, as you put it?" she asked, probing deeper into Jessie's thoughts.

"There was one, not so long ago," Jessie replied, with a softening of his voice. "He had lost his mind. I tried to reason with him, but he was in another world than me. I pleaded with him to stop what he was doing, but there was no reasoning with him. I waited until I basically saw the flash of light from the muzzle of his rifle before I fought back. Sometimes I wonder if I should have just let him take me. He wasn't a bad man. He had just been beaten down by this world to the point that he had no ability to see what was really around him anymore. Perhaps the world would have been better off with him in it today instead of me? I dunno. I acted in self-defense, but it sure doesn't make it easier to know that."

"It sounds to me as if he wanted out of this world, too."

"Maybe so," Jessie replied. Changing the subject, he pointed up ahead and said, "There it is, we're almost there. I just need to check on one thing before we lie low for the day."

"What? Where? The cemetery?" she asked, unsure of what Jessie was pointing out.

"Yeah, in that mausoleum to the left of the front gates. That's where I left Jack and Rosa," Jessie said, noticing that Leina was giving him a strange look. "It's another one of those long story things. Hopefully, we will live long enough for me to catch you up on everything," he said with a crooked smile.

As they approached the cemetery, the sun was now over the horizon, and the night had fully given way to a magnificent morning. Pointing to an old abandoned seventies-era pickup truck on the side of the road, Jessie said, "Take up an over-watch position from the bed of that truck. That old aluminum camper top on the back should allow you a decent view while staying out of sight. I'm gonna slip on over to the mausoleum to check on Jack and Rosa."

Turning toward the old truck, Leina paused and said, "Be careful."

Answering with only a smile, Jessie worked his way to the cemetery, taking cover along the way where he could. Upon reaching the cemetery gates, he stayed low, using the surrounding headstones as visual cover.

Reaching the mausoleum where he had left Jack and Rosa, he whispered softly, “It’s me, Jessie,” but heard no reply. Peeking in the front door, Jessie pushed it open to find no trace of them, other than footprints on the dusty old granite floor. With mixed emotions, he slipped out of the mausoleum and worked his way slowly to Leina’s position. As he neared the truck, he signaled for her to exit and join him and led her away from the cemetery, south toward the Rodeo Grill restaurant, which appeared to have long since been abandoned.

Stopping just short of Sumner Avenue, Jessie said, “I’ll cover you while you cross. Once you get on the other side, check the area, then wave me over while covering me. This wide open street will be one heck of a kill zone if anyone is watching.”

Nodding in the affirmative that she understood, Leina ran across Sumner Avenue, taking a position of both visual and physical cover behind an old, steel barbecue smoker built onto a pull-behind trailer that was located within the restaurant’s parking lot. Waiting a moment while scanning for threats, Leina waved Jessie across, where he joined her behind the smoker.

“Well, what did you find? Are they gone?” she asked.

“They aren’t there. There’s no sign of them. But on the bright side, there is also no indication of a struggle. There are no spent shell casings on the ground or anything else to indicate that they were taken by force. I’m just gonna stay positive for now and assume they slipped away to get Jack the medical attention he so desperately needed.”

Looking around, Leina asked, “Now what? We can’t just keep creeping around in broad daylight.”

"Let's try to find a way inside this old restaurant. It looks like it's been vacant for some time."

"Yeah, I would imagine it became hard to get the Sysco truck to bring supplies after it all started falling apart," Leina added.

"Is that a sense of humor, or sarcasm?" Jessie asked. "Either way, it's good to see you coming out of your shell."

"I'm just trying to keep my mind occupied to avoid thinking about unwanted things. You can call that whatever you want," she said, leaving Jessie's position while slipping in between the building and two rusty, old fly-infested commercial trash receptacles.

Joining her alongside the building, Jessie noticed that the back door by the dumpsters had been pried open, and the lock busted. "I'd say this place was ransacked for food quite some time ago, which sucks because I'm getting pretty dang hungry."

"Me, too. I could eat a horse," she replied as she held the door open while Jessie slipped inside with his rifle at the low ready, prepared to engage any possible threats that might lie in wait.

Nodding for her to follow, he said, "I just happen to know where one is. His name is Eli. He'd probably be tough and gristly, though."

"What?" she asked with a confused expression on her face.

"A horse. I know where one is if you're that hungry."

"Oh, shut up," she replied. "I could never do that."

"Then you've simply yet to get that hungry," Jessie said as he leaned his rifle against the wall and slipped behind the counter.

"What are you doing?" she asked.

"Like you, I'm sure this place has been cleaned out. But I'd be a fool to not at least try to find something," Jessie said as he rummaged through each of the drawers, cabinets, and underneath the counter. "Just keep an eye out while I look."

Walking over to the heavily tinted and dust covered window, Leina patiently watched the street for any signs of activity when she heard Jessie say, "Jackpot!"

Turning to see what the excitement was all about, she asked, "What? Did you find food?"

"Yep. They're like mini MREs. There are dozens of them. Do you prefer ketchup or mustard?" he said as he tossed her a small packet of ketchup.

Seeing the disappointed look on her face, Jessie added, "Hey, don't knock it. Ketchup is basically tomatoes, sugar, and salt. That'll help keep you alive until something better comes along. If nothing else, it'll give your taste buds something to do."

Tearing the packet open and sucking out the contents, Leina nodded in agreement and turned her attentions back to her view of Sumner Avenue, which passed just in front of the building.

Walking back around from behind the counter, Jessie joined Leina and said, "We're kind of in a hotspot, here. We should see some activity that gives us an idea of what move to make next. The county courthouse is in view from here. That's where they were keeping Rosa. And city hall is just a few blocks over that way," he said, pointing toward the northeast. "One way or another, we should be able to get a good view of Peronne's activity from here while we rest up."

"I'll take the first watch this time," Leina said. "I've got a lot on my mind and probably couldn't sleep, anyway."

"I'll take you up on that," Jessie said. "Dozing off for a few moments last night was the first sleep I've gotten in days."

Walking to the pantry area, Jessie looked around for a suitable place to take a nap. Finding a shelf that was previously used to store bread, Jessie said, "This will work. Wake me when it's my turn to take the watch."

"Will do," replied Leina as she gazed out the window, taking a seat in a corner booth in the restaurant's seating area.

## Chapter Thirty-One

As he sat high on the hill, feeling the breeze blow across his face as he looked his rifle over, he thought, *This old girl is starting to show some saddle wear. It's time to clean her up a bit.*

His thoughts interrupted by a distress-filled *baaa*, Jessie looked down the hill to see his sheep begin to scatter—all except for one. A lone mother ewe and her lambs were cornered by a pack of hungry wolves that circled them, slowly inching their way closer to her as her lambs cowered beneath her.

Immediately bringing his rifle to bear, Jessie placed the crosshairs of his scope on what he assumed to be the alpha-male, clicked off the safety, and...

"Jessie. Jessie, wake up," Leina said as she shook his arm. "Peronne is up to something."

Sitting up quickly, hitting his head on the empty bread storage shelf just above him, Jessie shouted, "Damn it! Ah, man," as he rubbed his head. "What? What is it?"

"Peronne is up to something. It sounds like he's taunting you over the radio. He keeps making sheep noises. It's quite creepy."

"He's probably just trying to goad me into replying so he can DF our position," Jessie said as he climbed down off the shelf and stretched.

"No, it's more than that, I'm afraid. I heard what sounded like a little girl crying in the background."

"Son-of-a-b—," Jessie responded with defeat in his voice as he began to pace around the room anxiously.

"What do you want to do?" she asked.

"I want to kill him. I want to kill them all. The only problem is we have no advantage when we do things on his terms. Our victories have defied their numbers by hitting them when they don't see it coming. If we walk into a scenario of their design, well, things would be different."

"Have you ever wondered if we, and you in your travels before you met me, have had victories because what we're doing is right?"

Sluffing off her comment, Jessie replied, "Being right doesn't give you an advantage. You and I have both seen plenty examples where doing what is right just gets you and your loved ones killed. No, I don't think God is intervening here. I believe he watched as humanity made our bed, now he's letting us sleep in it for a while. I know he's there, but I don't feel as if he's going to intervene. I've seen enough to know that's the case, and like I said, so have you."

"Being right might not get you anywhere, but being a pessimist doesn't either," she replied tersely.

"I'm not being a pessimist. I'm being a realist. Some people see their glass as half empty; others see their glass as half full. I see mine as being half-full of piss. And right now, Peronne is the one pissing in it. And that, I intend to stop."

"What do you propose?"

"Well, they've suffered numerous losses over the past few days, that we know for a fact. We know their morale has to be at an all-time low. That's our only advantage at this point. We have to continue to disrupt their freedom of movement and their perceived dominance of the battle space in order to undermine their only advantage, which is their unity of command."

Pausing to search for his words, Jessie concluded, saying, "As much as I hate to say it, as much as I hate to even propose it, I think we need to split up and divide their attention across the town. If we give them only one target to hit, both of us being together, they'll be able to focus and coordinate their strength accordingly. If we hit them from different places at different times, we will keep them reacting instead of advancing. As long as they are in a defensive mode, we may stumble across an opportunity to act. Without greater numbers, and without any real intelligence to go on, that's our only option as I see it."

"If you're hesitant to propose it because you don't think I can handle myself out there alone, you are sorely mistaken," Leina said with a stern voice and a serious, almost offended expression.

With a chuckle, Jessie replied, "No. No, that's not it at all. Trust me. I'm a little scared of you myself. I just think we make a good team. That, and as much as I've become used to being a lost soul in the world, it's nice to have a little humanity around at times. But you're right. We can both handle ourselves out there, so that's the best thing we can do right now, I think."

"It's all we have," she said as she gathered her things, placing a handful of ketchup packets into a bag. "I'm taking a few of your mini-MRE's," she said with a smile.

"Help yourself," he replied. "You tell me where you plan on going, and I'll work myself around the other way."

"I was thinking I will head a few blocks south and circle around town to the west. I'll find some havoc to wreak somewhere along the way to draw their attention. Once you see them reacting, you do the same on the northeast side of town. They won't know which direction to focus on. If we're lucky, at least one of us will survive this battle of attrition and make it to Peronne."

With a smile, Jessie chuckled, earning him a look of disdain from Leina. "No. No, I'm not laughing at you," he said with his hands up. "I'm laughing because you're basically a much better-looking version of me."

Returning the smile, she replied, "You're not so bad to look at yourself. Except for that dirty old beard. It looks like something scraggly with the mange died on your face."

"Oh, low blow. Well, you can't exactly receive your Dollar Shave Club razor supply in the mail once a month these days, you know."

"I was only messing with you," she replied.

"Finally, a sense of humor," Jessie said, warmly. "Now, don't go getting yourself killed. You're starting to grow on me."

"You do the same," she replied as she slipped out the door with her rifle in hand and a small sling-style bag over her shoulder.

As he watched her slip off into the surrounding area, quickly disappearing behind a small storage shed, Jessie said aloud to himself, "Please don't get yourself killed today."

## Chapter Thirty-Two

With his gear slung over his shoulder and his rifle in hand, Jessie left the relative safety of the Rodeo Grill and worked his way east down Sumner Avenue, doing his best to avoid being seen, before turning north to make his way around the city opposite of Leina's intended route. Slipping through the alley between the old Dollar store and the movie theater, Jessie stealthily crossed Main Street and slipped off into the brush to follow the Fort Sumner Main Canal back around to the west. He hoped to arrive on the north edge of town at the center of the city's geographic area before beginning his campaign of harassment and intimidation.

Pausing for a moment to sit and observe in a large stand of brush and weeds along the canal, Jessie began to sorely miss his AR-10 and its magnified optic. The Aimpoint CompM4 red dot optic on the rifle he had acquired from one of Peronne's men was fine for close quarters battle where rapid sight acquisition was critical, but he greatly missed the enhanced reconnaissance his magnified rifle scope provided him. *One of those bastards probably has my rifle, now. Hell, I'll probably get shot with it today. Whoever has it is far better off than I am with this puny little 5.56mm AR-15.*

After half an hour of seemingly calm silence, Jessie worked his way further west, still following the cover provided by the brush and trees along the banks of the canal, until reaching what he felt was the geographic midpoint of town. Scanning the area to look for threats and opportunities, Jessie saw a funeral home that appeared to still be in operation.

"That figures," he said to himself aloud. "Of all the businesses that closed, Lord knows a funeral home is probably still in high demand these days. Business will be booming after today if I can help it. The thing is, I hope I get to choose their customers for them."

Remaining in place and observing for another half an hour, Jessie heard a faint radio transmission through the police radio he carried. Turning up the volume slightly, he heard Peronne's voice saying:

*Hey, Shepherd! We had a little lamb to slaughter, but we found something better. Something you might have an interest in. She's a fine young thing. Dark hair, brown eyes, and curves that any man, including myself, just can't look away from. If I'm not mistaken, she knows you, too.*

As Jessie's thoughts raced through his mind, he wondered, *Is it Leina or Angela? Hell, they could both fit that description.* Maintaining his radio discipline, fighting off the urge to respond to Peronne's taunts, Jessie patiently waited for more information to be presented.

After a few moments, Peronne's voice came over the radio once again, saying:

*I'm disappointed in you, Shepherd. I thought Leina might have meant something to you, but I guess she's not a member of your flock. Oh well, we will have fun with her while she lasts, which may not be long with what we have in mind. You just keep hiding out there like the coward you are while we have our fun.*

Unsure if Peronne was trying to con him, Jessie held his silence, until hearing a struggle in the background, followed by Leina's voice, screaming:

*Kill these sons-of-b—! Kill them all. Send them all to hell to meet their friends! Don't worry about me, I'll...*

As her pleas were silenced, Peronne's voice came back over the radio, saying:

*I have to admit. The fire in this one is quite the turn-on. You'd better hurry if you want whatever's left.*

Disregarding his own better judgment, no longer caring if he gave his own position away, Jessie held the radio up to his face, and with a clenched jaw, said:

*If you harm her, I won't just kill you, I'll torture you. I'll send you to hell screaming for mercy. I will do things that even an evil, sadistic son-of-a-b— like yourself could never imagine.*

Keying up the microphone, Peronne replied in a flat, even voice:

*Here's the deal: we're not going to negotiate. This is my offer, and you can take it or leave it. As a matter of fact, I kind of hope you turn me down so that I can have my fun with her, and then hunt you down and kill you. That's a win-win. But because I'm a gentleman, I'll let you have some say in the matter, if you choose to accept. I'll trade you her, for you. Show yourself and turn yourself in to any of my officers, and I will let her go. You have my word on that.*

In reply, Jessie pressed the push-to-talk button, and said:

*"Bullsh—! Your word? How can anyone take you at your word? You've betrayed everyone around you every single day. You lie, you cheat, you steal from those who don't have the strength to fight back. You've aligned yourself not with your fellow citizens, but with the cartels and organized crime figures that helped to topple what was once a great nation. Your word isn't worth the spit that flies out of your fat, piggish mouth when you give it. I will gladly give myself to you in exchange for her freedom and safety, but you'll do it on my terms. You're not so powerful as you let on or you wouldn't be trying to strike a deal to save your own a— right now, so you had better listen up, because I'm only going to say this once. I will show myself from a semi-secure location, but only after one, and only one, of your men escorts Leina safely outside of town. Once I show myself, your man will leave her with the vehicle and a full tank of gas, and he will begin to walk back to town while she drives away. She will not be followed. Once she is on her way, I will lay down my rifle, and I will walk to you of my own accord and surrender myself as a trade for her. You have my word, and my word is worth something."*

After a momentary pause, Peronne answered over the radio with a perturbed voice:

*So be it! You've got one hour to get yourself to the east end of town for the trade. If you don't show up exactly on time and make contact, I'll kill her right there for the world to see. Do you understand me?*

Keying the microphone once again, Jessie replied:

> *Southwest end of town. You be on Sumner Avenue short of the Pecos River. I had better not see any of your men, other than her escort, on the other side of the river. No negotiations. You're not in charge here. It will be the southwest end of town. I'll see you in four hours. Don't double cross me, Peronne. You know I have the means to kill you. You know that, or you wouldn't be open to negotiations. Now, don't you dare say another word. Just shut your mouth and meet me at the west end of town in four hours. Leina better be unharmed, or there will be hell to pay.*

As silence fell over the airwaves, Jessie begrudgingly began to work his way westerly along the bank of the canal. All he could think about was her safety, and how he knew the world would be a better place with someone like Leina in it, rather than himself. He could see something special in her, and he knew her usefulness to mankind had yet to be fulfilled. To him, it was a worthy trade to make, and if he was going to die, at least it would be with purpose.

## Chapter Thirty-Three

As Peronne as his men gathered on the southwest end of Fort Sumner, just shy of the Pecos River like Jessie had instructed, Peronne nodded to the officer who had been assigned the task of escorting Leina out of town to bring her out of the running SUV. "I want him to be able to see her," Peronne said. "I want to lure that bastard out here so we can end this."

Shouting at him in response, Leina screamed aloud, "The only thing that's gonna come to an end is your reign of terror, you filthy son-of-a-b—!"

Raising his hand to strike her to silence her, the officer stopped short as Peronne shouted, "No! He's probably watching. Maintain your bearing, at least for now."

"Yes, Chief," the man replied.

Looking at his watch, Peronne mumbled to the man beside him, "Why is this bastard making me wait all day?"

"He's probably stalling like a coward," the man replied.

"Are you stupid?" Peronne asked rhetorically. "Have you been blind to everything going on around you? That man is no coward. He's a menace to our situation here, but he's no coward."

Simply nodding in agreement, the man went back to scanning the area with his binoculars in search of any sign of the man they knew only as the Shepherd.

As beads of sweat rolled down Peronne's forehead under the sun as it had passed the high noon position and was now traveling toward the western horizon, Peronne began to become impatient and irritated. "Come on. Come on! Show yourself!" he shouted.

All of his men were starting to show signs of weariness and fatigue from the stress and events of the past several days.

Peronne could feel his once iron grip of control beginning to loosen over his men. Peronne himself had bags under his eyes from the sleepless nights Jessie and Leina's rampage had caused him.

As Peronne began to curse under his breath, the radio silence was broken as Jessie's voice came over the radio at exactly four hours to the minute from when his demands were made.

*Hand her the radio. I need to verify if you are holding up to your end of the deal. Just keep your mouth shut and give her a radio.*

Nodding to the officer next to Leina, the man handed her the radio from his own duty belt, saying with a devious smile, "Your boyfriend wants to hear your voice. You must be good."

One of the other officers present, who had taken several shifts guarding her when she was drugged and unconscious, spoke up and said, "Oh, she is. I can attest to that."

Biting her tongue, attempting to hold her rage inside, Leina took the radio, and said, "Jessie?"

*Yeah, it's me. Are you okay?*

"I'm fine, but you can't do this. You can't. You know what you have to do."

"That'll be enough of that!" Peronne shouted. "Just answer him that you are okay, and we are holding up our end of the bargain and nothing more, or we will kill you right here for him to see."

Putting the radio back up to her mouth, she said, "They told me that one man would escort me out of town with a full tank of gas, and that once you showed yourself to them, they would let me go."

*Is it full? The tank, that is?*

"Yes, they showed me," she answered.

*Does it look like a trap for you, or do you think you'll be able to be on your way?*

"Everything looks like a trap these days and probably is. But there is gas in the car, that's all I know for sure. Just don't do it, please!"

Taking the radio from her, the officer nodded to Peronne as Peronne began to speak to Jessie "Okay, you talked to her. You verified that I'm holding up my end of the deal, now show yourself."

*Not until she is safely away from town, remember?*

Waving them away, the officer put Leina in the driver's seat of the vehicle while he held his pistol to her head, and said, "Okay, drive. Go straight down the road exactly one half mile on the odometer, and stop. When you do, put the vehicle in park, and wait."

Complying with his demands, Leina placed the transmission of the Chevrolet Suburban SUV into gear and began driving. Crossing the river, she looked into the rearview mirror as the town of Fort Sumner and Peronne's men got further and further away. She hadn't been outside of the borders of town since she was first ambushed. Her emotions were bittersweet. She desperately wanted to press the accelerator to the floor and speed away, never looking back, but she also wanted to stand and fight with Jessie, even if it cost her own life.

"That's far enough," the officer in the vehicle said. Still holding the gun on her, he ordered, "Put the transmission in park and shut off the engine."

Doing as he had instructed, the officer then said, "Don't try anything; we can still reach you from here. Understand?"

Replying with only a nod, Leina sat perfectly still in the vehicle while the man exited. He kept his pistol on her with his right hand while he held his radio in his left, awaiting Peronne's further instructions.

Peronne picked up his radio, and said, "Okay, 'Jessie,' I believe she said it is. Show yourself and we'll let her go. That's the deal."

After a brief moment of silence, one of Peronne's men said, "There! There he is!" as he pointed to the north as Jessie appeared from behind an old, rusty, metal building. "He's alone."

Verifying what the man had said with binoculars, Peronne said over the radio, "Drop your weapon."

As they watched Jessie raise his radio to his mouth from a distance, they heard through their speakers:

> *Tell the officer with Leina to toss his gun onto the seat of the SUV and tell her to drive away. Then, and only then, I'll drop my weapon.*

With anger in his voice, Peronne keyed the mic and said, "I'm not going to disarm one of my men with you standing there armed, posing a threat."

*Do it. That's the last thing I'm going to say,* Jessie said as he visibly tossed the radio to the side, out of his own reach, ending the conversation.

Shouting over the radio, Peronne said, "G— damn it! Give the b— your f— gun and start walking!"

Reluctantly doing as he was ordered, the man tossed his pistol onto the passenger seat of the vehicle, and before closing the door, he said, "We'll see you soon, b—," as he turned away from her and began walking back toward town.

Her heart conflicted, Leina looked over to the gun in the seat next to her, pressed the accelerator, and began to drive away as tears streamed down her face.

Knowing that Jessie no longer held his radio, Peronne screamed as loudly as he could with a voice full of rage and authority, "Now drop your f— gun!"

As he watched Leina drive away, a trail of dust following her onto Highway 60, Jessie tossed his AR15 to the side and began the long and dreaded walk toward Peronne and his men.

A devious smile grew over Peronne's face as a man standing to his side asked, "Do you want the sharpshooter to take him, sir?"

"No!" Peronne insisted. "We're going to have fun with this. Why end it too soon? Don't worry, you'll each get your turn."

"Should I send the others to get the woman yet?" the man then asked.

"No, let him get a little closer. After they bring her back, we'll let him watch for a while as you each take your turn with her."

As Jessie neared Peronne's position, his men began to form a circle around him, slowly and steadily closing in.

"So nice of you to join us on this lovely day. Now, put your hands on top of your head and drop to your knees," Peronne demanded.

Doing as he was ordered, Jessie lowered himself to the ground, one knee at a time, with a look of total defeat on his face.

With a satisfied smile on his face, Peronne nodded to one of the men behind Jessie, signaling him to approach him from behind, while he leaned over the man next to him, saying, "Now, send your boys to go get the b— and bring her back."

Looking at Peronne with rage and contempt, Jessie shouted, "You dirty son-of-a-b—!"

Laughing aloud, Peronne said, "What? You said it yourself, my word isn't worth the spit that flies out of my mouth when I speak it, or something to that effect. You should have known better."

Interrupting Peronne's victorious moment, the man said, "Uh... Chief."

"What? What is it?" barked Peronne.

"She's coming back."

"They got her already? Damn, that was fast."

"No, sir. She's driving back herself and at a pretty high rate of speed."

With Peronne and all of his men turning their attention to the trail of dust following the rapidly approaching SUV, Peronne shouted, "Kill the b—!"

As the officers opened fire, Jessie dove to his right shoulder and rolled onto his back, drawing his old Colt Peacemaker from a concealed position underneath his clothing. Quickly cocking the hammer of the old single-action revolver, he fired a shot, striking the man approaching him from behind directly in the forehead, the projectile smashing through the back of his skull.

As gunfire erupted all around him, Jessie expected to be struck with the burning impact of a bullet at any minute, only to realize that Peronne's men were dropping like flies around him, returning fire in all directions.

Quickly looking around, trying to make sense of what he was seeing with his own eyes, Jessie saw several of the townspeople firing from hidden positions all around. His heart nearly erupted with emotion as the good people of Fort Sumner were standing up to Peronne and his men. At this point, Jessie didn't care if he lived or died. This moment alone had made his life well-lived.

Snapping back to reality, Jessie saw Peronne run for one of the SUVs and peel away with the tires spinning wildly, throwing dirt and rocks as he fled.

Sprinting toward one of the remaining vehicles, Jessie dodged a poorly aimed, panicked shot made by one of Peronne's men, and returned fire, striking the man directly in the chest, dropping him to the ground.

Jumping into the vehicle, Jessie threw the SUV into gear and sped off in pursuit of Peronne, chasing the trail of dust he had left in his wake.

"F— coward!" Jessie shouted aloud as he drove like a mad man.

Speeding down Sumner Avenue at over one hundred miles per hour, Peronne barely slowed down enough to take the sharp turn onto 17th Street, sliding the SUV completely sideways and nearly losing control.

Making a well-controlled turn, Jessie was able to gain a little ground on Peronne, who was still far ahead of him.

Realizing where Peronne was heading, Jessie said to himself, "The airport! He's making a run for the airport!"

Speeding out of town on 17th Street, Peronne jerked the vehicle violently to the right, exiting the pavement, crashing through the airport's perimeter fence, speeding onto and across a taxiway, and then onto Runway 3, accelerating to well beyond one hundred miles per hour.

Following suit, Jessie nearly lost control as his SUV hit a large dip in the terrain, bouncing him, without a seatbelt, head first into the ceiling of the vehicle.

Regaining control and focus, Jessie maintained his pursuit, following Peronne onto the runway, accelerating to the SUV's maximum speed in an attempt to regain lost ground.

Smoke bellowed from Peronne's tires as he applied maximum braking pressure and yanked the vehicle off the runway, heading toward the general aviation hangars.

Maintaining his pressure on Peronne, Jessie slid his SUV sideways in an attempt to make the last minute turn. The vehicle slid off the pavement and into the dirt and grass, losing control, and nearly rolling the SUV on its top as it spun around wildly. Catching traction mid-slide, the tires were side loaded, skipping across the ground, coming to rest on all four wheels, facing the wrong direction, causing Jessie to lose valuable ground on Peronne.

Resuming his chase, Jessie saw Peronne's SUV in front of a large aircraft hangar, noticing that the hangar doors had been opened just enough for a man to slip through. Knowing he stood too great a chance of walking directly into an ambush, Jessie opted to park along the side of the building in order to enter the building from one of the side doors.

Stepping out of the vehicle, Jessie realized that in his haste to pursue Peronne, he had set out with nothing more than his Colt tucked into his waistband. "Damn it," he whispered to himself as he flipped the loading gate open and replaced the spent cartridge with a fresh one from his pocket.

Opening the door with his left hand, holding his Colt in his right, Jessie entered the hangar and listened carefully for any signs of activity. Slipping quietly through an abandoned aircraft avionics maintenance work center, Jessie looked out into the main hangar area, seeing several light GA aircraft, such as a Piper Seneca, a Beechcraft Baron, and a Cessna Skylane.

*Those airplanes aren't abandoned,* Jessie though, noticing the well-maintained and dust-free condition of the aircraft inside the hangar. Hearing a metallic thud from a wrench being knocked off a counter and bouncing off of the hard, concrete floor of the hangar, Jessie spun around just in time to see Peronne take aim with a twelve-gauge police issue shotgun.

Quickly diving behind a large maintenance cart, containing a hydraulic servicing unit, Jessie narrowly avoided being hit by the buckshot as it penetrated the hydraulic reservoir, spilling gallons and gallons of slippery, purple Skydrol hydraulic fluid onto the hangar floor.

Racking another round into the chamber of the Remington 870 pump-action shotgun, Peronne fired another shot blindly, keeping Jessie pinned down behind the metal cart while he ran across the back of the hangar and out the rear fire exit.

Leaving his position of cover, Jessie ran to the fire exit, and dashed out into the area behind the hangar, looking both ways, but seeing no sign of Peronne. *Damn it, 50/50 chance... left or right?* he quickly thought as he decided to run around the hangar to the left, in hopes of catching sight of Peronne before he was once again fired upon.

Reaching the west-facing outside wall of the hangar, Jessie heard a diesel generator fire up, followed immediately by the large electrically actuated doors on the front of the hangar beginning to open. Running on around the large structure to reach the main hangar doors, Jessie caught a glimpse of Peronne as he stood on the wing of the Beechcraft Baron and fired several volleys of buckshot at Jessie, forcing him to dive back behind the side of the building to seek cover.

Hearing both engines of the Baron cough and belch themselves to life as the propellers began to spin, Jessie rounded the corner, cocked the hammer and fired at the cockpit. Cocking the hammer and firing a second shot, Jessie saw a bright flash of muzzle blast as well as the accompanying crack of the shotgun's powerful muzzle report as Peronne fired the shotgun with one hand out the co-pilot side-entry door as he began taxiing the aircraft with his feet and free hand at the controls.

Speeding out of the hangar, wildly swerving the aircraft to the left and taxiing under what was near takeoff power, Peronne headed for the runway while Jessie fired the last remaining shots from his revolver, seemingly having no impact on the aircraft as it sped away.

Catching movement out of the corner of his eye, Jessie saw one of Peronne's SUVs rapidly approaching from across the airport, following the trail of destruction that Jessie and Peronne had left during their vehicular pursuit.

*Crap!* Jessie thought as he began to retreat toward the hangar while he simultaneously flipped open the loading gate on his pistol, ejecting the spent shell casings as he ran, in preparation to reload. Stopping just short of the hangar, Jessie saw a woman behind the wheel of the vehicle. "Leina!" he shouted as she came to a stop. To his surprise, he saw Angela exiting the vehicle from the passenger-side door, both of the women rushing toward Jessie.

Pointing at the escaping aircraft, Jessie shouted, "That's him! That's Peronne!

Turning back toward the SUV, Jessie watched as Angela pulled out her long-range precision rifle and ran as fast as she could, to get into a position to fire. As the aircraft reached takeoff speed and rotated into the air, Leina knelt down in front of Angela, who placed the barrel of her rifle onto Leina's shoulder to steady her shots while Leina covered her ears, took aim, and fired at the departing aircraft. Cycling the bolt, chambering another round, Angela fired again, and again, until her five-round box magazine was empty.

As the three of them watched Peronne fly away, the aircraft slowly began to list to the left, entering a left-wing-low turn, spiraling down to the ground. The aircraft was completely destroyed on impact, bursting into flames, with its wing-tanks full of volatile and highly flammable Avgas.

Jessie walked over to the two women, hugged them both, and then the three of them stood there and silently watched as Chief Peronne's wreckage burned into nothing more than a smoldering heap of twisted aluminum and ashes.

After several moments of silence, Jessie turned to Angela and Leina, and asked, "How? What?" as he tried to figure out how the two of them had joined forces to follow him in the pursuit.

Leina spoke up, saying, "I just couldn't drive away and leave you there to die. It would have haunted me for the rest of my life. I would have rather died, right there with you. By the time I got back, chaos had erupted as Angela here, and several other townspeople had begun to engage Peronne's men. She knew who I was. Evidently, everyone did. Anyway, we watched your trail of dust as you chased Peronne out of town, so we decided to follow."

Turning back to view the smoldering wreckage, Jessie said, "Thank God you did. Thank God you did..."

## Chapter Thirty-Four

Several weeks later...

As Jessie pushed his chair away from the dinner table at Jack's home, he looked at Angela and said, "That was a damn fine meal. The best I've had in, well, years."

"You're welcome. It's nice to have a semblance of normalcy around here again. I can't believe how fast the town seems to be recovering from the hell that Peronne put us through."

Looking to Jack at the head of the table, Jessie said, "Well, with Mayor McGuigan here in charge of things, I'm sure it'll all work out just fine. How exactly did you con the rest of the people here into giving you that job, Jack?"

"It's not something I was aspiring to be, trust me on that," he replied. "I just want to help get some legitimate local leadership established, and get a militia made up of all of the people, the entire population of able-bodied adults, up and running, so that we never run into a problem like Peronne again. We will never be disarmed again. We will never let anyone, elected or not, run roughshod over our individual, God-given rights, ever again."

"Amen to that," Jessie said, as he raised his glass with everyone in the room joining him for a toast.

That evening, after everyone had gone back to their own homes and retired for the night, Jessie sat on the front porch with Jack, quietly taking a sip of home-brewed beer, made by one of the locals. Breaking the silence, Jessie said, "I just wish Leina hadn't slipped away in the middle of the night like she did. I mean... I understand. She's never going to be able to rest in this world without trying to find her children, but she didn't have to go on her own."

"Now, Jessie, you know as well as I do, that sometimes people need to set out on their own for a mission that even they know, they probably won't complete. As a matter of fact, that sounds like the story of someone else I know," Jack replied, taking a sip of beer. "Damn, that's good stuff, all things considered."

Noticing that Jessie had suddenly become tongue-tied as he stared blankly at the wooden porch floor, Jack added, "As a matter of fact, it seems to me, like you've got such a thing stewing in your mind right now. You know, you don't have to leave. We just happen to have open, the position of sheriff, who will, of course, be our militia leader as well. Do you know anyone around here that has the qualifications to fill such a position? I think I might know someone who does."

Rocking his chair back and forth, patiently waiting on Jessie's reply, Jack asked, "So, Sheriff Townsend, do you know anyone who holds such qualifications?"

Looking up at Jack, Jessie replied, "Sheriff Townsend died a long time ago. I'm just Jessie, or J. T. now. And you're right, I know exactly how Leina must have felt when she left, leaving nothing but a goodbye note behind."

"You're not gonna leave a note, though, are you?" asked Jack.

"I... I've got to..."

Interrupting him before he could finish, Jack said, "I know, Jessie. I know. Your soul will never rest either, just like hers. Just promise me, if you ever find room in your heart to be a part of a community again, that you'll consider us here at Fort Sumner. We'd be honored and lucky to have you as one of our fellow citizens."

"Thanks, Jack. I'll always keep you good people in mind and in my heart. Take care of Angela, or rather, I guess I should tell her to take care of you."

With a laugh, Jack replied, “Yeah, that’s a more appropriate statement these days. She’s something else.”

“You did well, my friend. The world needs more parents like you, if we’re going to make it through all of this.”

Answering only with a smile, Jack tipped his glass and took another sip of beer, as he and Jessie gazed out at the stars, enjoying each other’s company, for what they both knew was the last time.

~~~ The End ~~~
~~~

## A Note from the Author

As I sit here before my keyboard, having completed my eighth book, I reflect upon what an amazing journey it has been. I've met a lot of people along the way, both in person and online, who have greatly inspired me to continue down this path. People from within the industry as well as readers have made this a true labor of love for me that I plan to continue for my foreseeable future. I thank you each and every one for that, from the bottom of my heart.

If I have not had the honor of making your acquaintance and if you like my work, please find me on Facebook at
http://facebook.com/stvbird
and at my blog at http://www.stevencbird.com. You can also follow me on Twitter at http://twitter.com/stevencbird. In addition, my Amazon author page can be found at http://www.amazon.com/Steven-Bird/e/B00LRYYBDU/ where you can see all of my available work.

I look forward to hearing from each and every one of you, and may God bless you and your loved ones in all of your future endeavors.

Just as Jack and Jessie shared a drink in the final chapter, I raise my glass to each and every one of you, and offer you my friendship and thank you for yours in return.

Respectfully,

Steven C. Bird

## About the Author

Steven Bird was born in Harlan, KY in 1973, where he lived until joining the U.S. Navy in 1992. He spent the next thirteen years living in Northwest Washington State, where he served on active duty for eleven of those years. After leaving active duty, he completed twenty years of service in the Navy Reserve retiring as a Navy Chief Petty Officer. While in the reserves, he pursued a civilian flying career, serving as a flight instructor, charter pilot, turboprop first officer, jet first officer, jet airline captain, and he currently flies as the captain of a super-midsized business jet based out of Knoxville, Tennessee. He has served in both military and federal law enforcement capacities and holds CFI, CFII, MEI, and ATP pilot certificates with numerous jet type ratings, as well as a bachelor's degree in eBusiness.

In his spare time, Steven has been involved in off-road motorcycle racing, competitive shooting, hunting, fishing, hiking, and myriad other outdoor activities. He currently focuses his free time on his family as a happily married father of three. He and his wife Monica have a farm in Deer Lodge, Tennessee, where they raise their own fruits and vegetables, in addition to raising chickens, Katahdin sheep, American Blackbelly sheep, and various breeds of cattle.

Steven Bird is a self-sufficiency-minded individual with a passion for independence and individual liberty. He puts this passion into his writing where he conveys the things that he feels are important in life, intertwined with action-packed adventure and the struggles of humanity.

47138050R00141

Made in the USA
San Bernardino, CA
25 March 2017